# I AM KEATS

# I AM KEATS

## THE ART OF INCITING CHAOS

TOM ASACKER

SHANNON MCCARTHY-MINUTI

ISBN-13: 978-1546431305
ISBN-10: 1546431306


Printed in the United States of America
First Edition: 2017
Library of Congress Cataloguing in Publication Data:
A catalog record for this book is available from the
Library of Congress


Book cover design by Bukovero

*To you, the spirited few, who dance to the secret song inside of you.*

# Contents

*One must still have chaos in oneself
to be able to give birth to a dancing star.*

FRIEDRICH NIETZSCHE

# Tolstoy and the Blues

*eo Tolstoy wasn't a bluesman. But he knew that secret place of melancholy. He had the blues in his cold Russian veins. Tolstoy was the one who said that all happy families are alike. But every unhappy family is unhappy in its own way.*

*The blues are about secrets and lies. About pain and morphine. About love lost, and love never found. About too many bills and not enough money. The blues are the rhythm of your mother's heart when you are in the womb. They are the brothers who cannot speak of loss and regret but instead hide behind the roles they have adopted. The blues are subversive and spiritual. I might never meet God. But sometimes I think I hear him in a riff. The blues are*

*the stuff of Tolstoy, and B.B. King. And Lady Day. And Etta. Can't ever forget Etta.*

*B.B. King said that as long as people have problems, the blues will never die. I think he and Tolstoy might have gotten along. They would have found common ground in this simple truth: Life will bring you to your knees. And only you—how much heart you have, how much soul, how much blues in your veins—will decide whether you stand up again.*

*You have asked me to write a conservatory application essay answering the question: What people or events inform your music and why?*

*This is actually a very complicated question. So I am going to tell you the honest truth. Parts of this story will sound like I am making it up. But just like the blues, you'll have to listen to my story with your soul.*

*My name is Kyle Anderson, and I may be a white boy from Cali, but me, Tolstoy, B.B., Lady Day, Etta, Buddy Guy... we all know about that place where you have no choice but to look inward and find the song of your life.*

*It all started not that long ago. But before I tell you this tale, I guess I need to tell you what we were all like before. Before our lives were turned upside down.*

*It started on Monday. My father worked late at the studio; the animated movie his team was working on was somehow not what he had envisioned. And there's this unspoken rule that no one is allowed to leave work before Peter Anderson. Well, except for Sam. His assistant. And that's only because (a) she knows when to let what my dad says go in one ear and out the other, and (b) he'd be lost without her. She once told me she was the remora fish—and he was the Great White shark. Perfect symbiosis.*

*Dad came home late, as usual, popped into my room for about thirty seconds to ask me how my homework was going, and headed into his home office. He's trained himself to only need five hours of sleep. Something about Einstein and Edison not needing a lot of sleep.*

*But really? I think he was afraid to sleep.*

Peter Anderson stared at the ceiling, trying again to shake off the nightmare, the horror wrenched out of time. Thirty years later, give or take, and it still took over his nocturnal mind at least once a month.

It pissed him off.

He couldn't change the outcome. He could relive that nightmare every night until he was a very old man, and *still* nothing would change. So why waste so much as a single brain cell on something that was already determined? Done. Finished. *Dead and buried.*

He rolled over and exhaled a sigh. Taking the remote from the bedside table, he pressed "open," and the blackout shades parted, revealing his million-dollar view of the Valley and letting in the grey sunshine—grey because his bedroom windows were tinted.

He replaced the remote, and then, like the invisible pull of a magnet, he opened the top drawer of his nightstand. He reached in, the picture where it always was. He pulled it out, and in the moody dawn light, he stared at the four of them. His mother and father sat on the top step of their home, he and his brother Phil perched in the middle between them. His mother leaned her head to the right in toward her boys, his father leaned his in left. He and Phil were grinning—Phil missing his front teeth. Peter was taller and lanky, the beginnings of a growth spurt. But the boys could pass as twins. Not anymore of course.

He couldn't remember his parents any longer. Not in any real way. He couldn't hear their voices. He used to try to commit her voice to memory, singing in this off-key way she had, like she didn't care who listened, who heard each crack as she tried to imitate Joni Mitchell.

He had one memory of them, dancing in the kitchen, as if he and Phil weren't there, this connection between the two of them like some thread tied her heart to his father's. And then, just like the nightmare, it all culminated in screeching tires, shattered glass, crumpled metal. And then it was just him.

And Phil.

He shoved the picture in his nightstand where it belonged. He sat up and padded into his bathroom, removing his white silk pajamas, custom-made by his bespoke Hong Kong tailor. His shower could fit his entire executive team, comfortably, with rainforest sounds that tripped on, and nozzles and rain-shower spouts that pummeled the angry knots in his shoulders and neck from every direction. He always finished with two minutes of biting cold water, bracing himself, in some way, preparing him for a day of nonstop decisions and pressure.

He dried off with two—always two—Turkish bath towels he had his assistant Sam order from Harrod's in London. He'd experienced the silky foutas in a hotel in Madrid and had Sam track them down.

He walked into his closet and pressed a remote control switch stored in the center island. His suits slowly moved along a rod, organized by color and fabric. He selected a charcoal Hugo Boss. Tasseled Italian loafers. A silk tie washed pale like a watercolor. Subtle diamond cufflinks. His initials embroidered on the cuffs of his crisp blue shirt.

He stared at himself in the mirror. His pale eyes were difficult to read. He leaned closer to the mirror. *Who was that guy with the silver hints at the temples?*

He threw his shoulders back and flashed a smile. The best cosmetic dentist in L.A. had ensured what he knew the interns in his office called his "movie star smile." He waited for the smile to reach his eyes, but it didn't. It hadn't in a very long while. But no matter, when his green eyes went stormy, he knew they instilled a shot of resolve in everyone in the office. His team would scramble and come together, happily burning the midnight oil.

And *that* was the key to making his studio number one. Peter found the best people, then demanded their personal best and accepted nothing less. And

LeRoy Neiman-like painting of a smiling cartoon toaster was centered precisely on the wall. He looked down as he flipped his storyboards. Then he froze. On one storyboard, someone had drawn a cartoon toaster just like the one in his painting, but angry, with smoke coming out of it, and on a piece of popped toast, the word "jerk" burnt into its surface.

Peter blinked twice. He took a Sharpie and scribbled "WTF!" on the board. He *would* find out who drew this, and what they were thinking.

He grabbed his iPhone and angrily poked at his contacts list. He put it on speaker.

*"Hello, this is Sam! I am currently having an out-of-office experience. Leave a message after the beep. And if this is Peter, at least wait until I've had a cup of coffee."*

As Peter waited for the beep, a reminder popped up on his screen. This week was his brother's fortieth birthday.

*Beep.*

"Hey Sam, I don't really care what kind of experience you are having. I need those reports no later than nine. And find out for me who the last person was who worked on the storyboards. And…"

He shook his head and cleared his throat. "And… it's Phil's birthday. Again. Get him a gift card.

Maybe to that donut place. Dow's or Ducko's or whatever that greasy hole-in-the-wall is called."

He disconnected. He looked at the time. "Kyle! We're leaving. NOW!"

⁀

*If my father was a piece of music, a kind of music, he would be a march by John Phillips Souza. He would be precision and timing, and that loud brass and pomp and circumstance.*

*My Uncle Phil? He'd be the plaintive wail of Neil Young. Or any of the protest folk singers of the 1960s and 1970s. He would be the singers who were against the Man, against the War, against the Bureaucrats.*

*Me? Well, this was before everything crazy that followed. So I would just be me, trying to slide under the radar. I'd be the guy playing his guitar but instead of plugged into an amp, I'd be plugged into my Beats. Hearing the music I played in my head only. Not ready to play my song aloud.*

*But things were about to get discordant. Where none of us could hear our own notes. Just this cacophony of noise.*

⁀

Her voice came through the speakers.

"Sam, here. Who is this?"

"You know who this is."

"Sorry. Please identify yourself."

"Sam!"

"Sorry, Peter. What can I do for you, Fearless Leader?"

"I need to get a gift for Phil."

"I know. You already told me to get a gift card from Dow's, but I am refusing on principle."

Peter pressed on the intricate controls of his treadmill to slow it down and finally stop. "What do you *mean* you refuse on principle?"

"It's the big four-oh! The big one! You can't get him a donut shop gift card."

"You know my brother. He's a Philistine. Greasy spoon gift card—just what he wants."

"No. Come up with something better. He's your brother. Other than Kyle, he's your only living relative. Look at it this way: If you ever need a kidney, he's your best shot. So don't get him a measly *donut* gift card for his fortieth birthday."

"I didn't say be cheap about it. You can get him a five-hundred-dollar Dow's gift card."

"Again. Kidney versus donuts. I'm not seeing it."

Peter jumped off the treadmill and began doing squats. He stood abruptly. "I know just the thing."

"This should be good."

"Call up that adventure company. Get him and me an all-day mountain biking trip up the coast. It's perfect. Saturday is supposed to be gorgeous. I need some endurance training, anyway. Kill two birds with one stone."

"Um. Peter?"

"Yeah?"

"Have you *met* your brother? You're asking him to do intense biking?"

"Yeah. And since this is my weekend with Kyle, why don't you book him too?"

"Does Kyle like to bike?"

"Doesn't matter. Just do it, Sam."

"Sure thing. But I'm just letting you know, I don't feel good about this gift."

"Duly noted. Good-bye Sam."

*Now, while Dad was coming up with the very worst gift a human being could have chosen for his brother, who had the general build of the Pillsbury Dough Boy, Uncle Phil was reporting to work. While Dad had the corner office at*

"A *what*?"

"Forget it."

"Look, exercise won't kill you. Now that you're turning forty, it's time you thought about it."

Phil shook his head. "Whatevs."

"Whatevs? What are you... thirteen?!"

"Is that all you needed from me? I should have clocked back on five minutes ago."

"Yeah. And is that Neil Young? Is that what I hear playing in the background?"

"Yeah, so?"

"Seriously? Can't you listen to something new? From *this* side of the millennium? Justin Bieber? Anything?"

"It's Pandora, asshole. It plays what 'it' likes to play. Unlike you, it has a mind of its own."

"Look, never mind. Just be ready for this bike trip, OK? I'll pick you up at eight."

"Eight what? A.M.?!"

"Yeah. A.M. So set your little antiquated clock radio."

"You know... you really don't have a *clue* who I am. Your assistant knows me better than you, my own brother."

"Please, don't start that shit with me today. Just be ready to go when I get there."

Phil closed his phone and tossed it onto the table. He kicked his feet up and leaned back, fingers interlocked behind his head.

"Whatever you say... *Dad*," he sneered at the phone.

Chester Simms, arms crossed over his chest, cleared his throat. After a moment, Phil snapped his head around.

Chester's face was turning beet red. "My office. Ten minutes."

⤙

*Roy Orbison, the guy with the angelic voice, had a song "Working for the Man." Uncle Phil called it "The Sheeple Song."*

*Uncle Phil was fired, right then and there in Chester's office. But he didn't care. He never liked working for "the Man." And most especially, he never liked working for a buffoon. He didn't like punching a clock. He didn't like thinking about money. He didn't like doing laundry. He didn't like anything mindless. He didn't want to be a Sheeple.*

*creatures in the wisps of white magical cotton that dotted the horizon.*

# Learning to Fly

mpty spaces. *Jazz, to me, is about acknowledging the empty space of one of the other guys in your quartet—like he plucks that bass, and then the drummer goes under the empty space just after, the breath, to lift it up—the half-beat between them. It's second nature to the best guys—and women. Man, ever listen to Ella? Be-bopping and scatting in the empty spaces. Or listen to Benny Goodman swing to Gene Krupa's drums? Or listen to Wynton Marsalis. When he plays his trumpet, he is playing it on the wind—in the spaces between notes somehow. The fabric of the Universe.*

*Watching my dad and Uncle Phil try to lead us—the three of us—on this bike trail was like watching Coltrane try to play with the Backstreet Boys. I mean, don't get me*

*wrong, blending harmonies and pop music has a place. But Coltrane? And them? A fancy word.*

*Disharmony.*

*Which meant the entire bike ride was discordant. We couldn't talk to each other. I didn't even try to butt in. I just watched as they talked over each other's empty spaces. They just couldn't see.*

*They just couldn't hear.*

～

"Keep up!" Peter shouted over his shoulder. *Idiot!* His brother's khakis were blowing in the wind, and occasionally snagging, causing Phil to almost tumble off.

Kyle brought up the rear. Peter was certain Kyle was embarrassed of Phil. Imagine if his son ran into someone from school? Phil looked like a homeless man on an $800 bike. No wonder Kyle held way back. What should have been a fun day was marred by Phil's sloppy appearance and bad attitude. And he clearly had no clue how to operate the gears.

"Big hill, guys! Don't jam on the front brakes…" He shot a glance behind him, then turned and looked in the mirrors mounted on his handlebars.

His brother was going to end up in a ditch. "*Keats!* Talking to you! Don't jam on the breaks!"

His brother, who was sweating like a frothy pig in a hot August pen, mocked in sing-song. "Don't jam on the front brakes…"

Peter winced. It was like watching a train about to wreck in slow-motion. "Seriously! You'll go right over the handlebars!"

And then Phil braked. There was the thwup-thwup sound of the hem of his left pant leg jamming into the bike's chain. Peter slowed down at the bottom of the hill, then pulled to the side just as his brother sailed over the handlebars, landing, thud, flat on his back.

Peter turned his bike around and screeched up beside him.

"What-did-I-tell-you?! Are you OK?"

Kyle pulled up. "Oh my God, Uncle Phil! That was scary. Are you OK?"

Phil's eyes were shut, but he eventually opened them. "Fine. Yup. Fine. Might need like a lot of ibuprofen tonight."

"So you didn't hear me tell you not to jam on your brakes? No one listens to me. *Story of my fucking life.* Get up and let's get going. We have a lot of trail left to cover."

Kyle climbed off his bike, grabbed Uncle Phil's hand, and helped him up. He opened his mouth to say something to Peter, but then seemed to think better of it.

"Ready, gentlemen? Let's go."

Phil and Kyle each climbed on their bikes. Phil started off after his brother, and then Kyle brought up the rear like before.

Peter chugged along up the next short hill. Phil worked hard to keep up, but the sun was high in the sky and sweat poured down his face and neck. Kyle was coasting in the back, headphones draped around his neck because of his bike helmet. Taking a hard breath, Peter slowed down and aligned his bike with Phil's.

"This is fun, huh?"

Phil slowed and wiped at his foggy glasses. "Oh, yeah. This is an effing laugh riot. A ball of fun. Happy birthday to me!"

"Come on. It reminds me of that time we rode to that country store. Remember?"

"Yup."

"Rode our bikes all that way. Got ice cream. Mom and Dad didn't even know we were gone."

"Sure we did."

"We didn't?" Peter shifted the gears on his mountain bike.

"We did, but we didn't get ice cream."

"Sure we did. You were too young to remember anyway—"

Phil braked and his tires skidded across the mountain trail. "That's it! I am done."

"Done?" Peter braked then dismounted. Kyle braked and stopped about twenty feet behind them.

Phil removed his helmet, which had been two sizes too big. He held it by the chinstrap and stalked toward his brother.

"God, you're fucking irritating. You don't even see it! You couldn't see your hand in front of your face." He held up his free hand and waved it in front of Peter's eyes.

"See what? I was reminiscing. You know... the good, old days. When our parents were alive, you selfish bastard."

Phil tossed his helmet to the ground. "Reminiscing?! That's not what happened! You're making it up as you go. Creating some *compelling*

40

narrative, like the fucking storyboards for your stupid movies. Well, I'm not a supporting actor in The Life Story of My Big Shot Brother."

"What? Who gives a shit? I don't remember it that way! Why does it even matter?"

"Well, I *do* remember it. Picture-perfect, like it happened yesterday, OK?! It's not enough you have to control my life, you have to control my memories, too?"

Peter snarled, "Who's controlling your life?!"

Phil threw his arms up and looked around. His face dripped sweat, and his damp *I am Keats* T-shirt stuck to his chest. "Look around! It's my birthday! Mine! What the hell are we doing here?!"

Peter looked back toward Kyle, who was staring down at the ground, lost in whatever world he was in. This was so typical of Phil. He was so annoying that he was alienating poor Kyle.

Watching his brother pace and snort like a bull about to charge, Peter quickly reached into his bike bag. He dug out a couple of sandwiches. "OK, bro... hold on."

He held up a perfectly wrapped sandwich to Phil and waved his hand at Kyle. "Lunch break."

Grabbing a cool bottled water from his insulated bag, Peter said, "Here. We're probably just both thirsty. Hungry. Low blood sugar... Eat the sandwich. You'll feel better."

Phil swiped it out of Peter's hand, plopped down on the ground, tore off the wrapping, and stuffed it into his mouth. Kyle approached and shook his head at a sandwich, grabbing a water instead, and sitting a few feet from his dad and uncle, stared out from a rock onto a tree-lined valley below.

Peter exhaled, sat down next to Phil and meticulously unwrapped his sandwich like an elderly aunt unwrapping a Christmas present, hoping to re-use the wrapping paper. *Thank God for chicken salad. Another Phil disaster averted.*

He took a bite of his sandwich, then a swig of cold water. Glancing at his brother, he smiled. "Beautiful day, huh?"

Phil, mouth full of sandwich, just shrugged and grunted.

Peter concentrated on his sandwich. He stared off at his son. "Wanna join us?" he shouted.

But Kyle's head popped to the eternal soundtrack. Peter started to wish he had never bought Kyle Beats. But he had told Kyle if his latest report card

Peter looked at Kyle, who was now sitting on the ground cross-legged, his head in his hands. He wanted to scream at his brother, but his son was here. Hell, if he was sixteen again, he might have knocked Phil on his ass. But he was better than that now. This was such utter ungrateful bullshit.

Peter stormed over to his bike, mounted it, and snapped at Kyle, "Let's go!" He started pedaling down the path. *Mindfulness Peter... breathe in. Breathe out. Deep... cleansing... breaths...*

Phil hustled to his bike and quickly followed.

Kyle shook his head and pulled on his own helmet.

Phil called over his shoulder to Kyle, "Just know none of this has anything to do with you, Kyle. This is between me and your dad. You're loved, dude."

Phil peddled furiously. He final caught up to Peter. "You can't even see it. You're the most successful, *miserable* prick in the world."

Phil dropped his head down and felt the heaviness of exhaustion as he tried to keep parallel with Peter. "Tell the truth! Do you even know who Keats was?"

Peter, in the most blasé voice he could muster while riding a bike, said, "John Keats. Nineteenth-century English Romantic poet. Shelley, Byron... *Coleridge*. Whatever, OK? You're unhinged."

"That's what I thought. You *know* Keats like you know everything. For its usefulness, its relevance to you. The center of the universe. You probably needed to memorize Keats and Coleridge for an exam, right Mr. Valedictorian? Mr. Hotshot CEO?"

"Uh-huh."

Peter pedaled harder, trying to pull away. Phil struggled, but with determination on his face, he caught up. "Your life's an abstraction, Petey."

"Don't call me that."

"Petey, don't you see what I am saying? All your Coleridge planning and controlling. You *think* you'll finally live life when you 'get there.' Bet you have a long bucket list full of exotic places, like hike Mt. Kilimanjaro. Scuba along the Great Barrier Reef. Surf off the coast of the Easter Islands."

"Yup."

"Well, guess what, smart guy? When you finally *get* there... you'll find there isn't any *there* there!"

*What the hell did he just say?* Peter bore down on the pedals, picking up speed. Enough was enough. It was time to shed his brother. He glanced in the rearview mirrors mounted on his handlebars and saw that sky, zooming toward the bridge before going aloft again.

Phil snapped his head skyward.

He wasn't paying attention to anything but that stupid bird. Like what kind of crazy person cared about a crow—they were trash eaters as far as Peter was concerned.

But Phil was just focused on the damn thing. It cawed. And Peter was certain Phil *cawed back*. God, he was the most embarrassing human on all of the earth.

Peter screamed to his brother, "Watch out!"

Oblivious, Phil's bike rolled on and smashed into the low bridge railing—hard. He heard a *crack* like a small explosion. And then, in a frozen moment of time, he watched helplessly as his brother—his only remaining living relative except for Kyle—sailed off toward the rocky riverbed below, as the crow cawed and hovered slightly before flying into the forest.

"911, what's your emergency?" The woman's voice was calm and efficient.

Peter grabbed at his hair. His white bike shorts were smeared with blood. He paced back and forth as Kyle knelt by Phil, tears in his eyes, frozen as he stared down at his uncle.

"We've had an accident on the Greenwood bike trail—" Peter found himself uttering a mantra under his breath. *PleaseGod, PleaseGod, PleaseGod.*

"OK, sir. What is your exact location?"

Peter knelt near Phil, fingering his brother's cracked bike helmet.

"Sir? Are you still there?"

But Peter was gone. He was there, but he was gone, into the nightmare. Into the truck headlights again. Into the crash. Into the world when it stopped making sense, when it went from four, from love and mother and father and two sons, to two. Just two. And now?

Kyle shook his father's arm. "Dad! The 911 lady is on speaker phone. Answer her."

Peter heard the sirens from far off, a wailing in his head that seemed to echo the deep pain in his soul. Peter was numb. Frozen. He shivered though the sun was high in the bright afternoon sky. Finally, Peter answered the woman, and knelt with Kyle, waiting for someone to come and save Phil. *Save him.* Unlike that night so long ago, when four became two. When their parents could not be saved. When the accident just some footnote. Some event that had no meaning.

Because weren't life and death—especially death—meaningless?

Shit. He didn't even know what he was saying or thinking anymore.

Time went by. Seemingly endless minutes. He had no idea of time—night or day. Hospitals were like casinos in that way.

"Peter!"

He turned. Ramona! He smiled slightly to himself, and fought at the rock that lodged in his throat. Funny how her arrival always made him feel as if everything would be all right—when right now, he had no idea if that was so or not.

She rushed toward him, fingering the cross on her neck in an unconscious way. She was dressed—as she always did now—in a business suit, perfectly tailored. She was sixty-something but looked twenty years younger. Her jet-black hair was cut in a sleek bob, and her warm caramel skin was without a wrinkle.

She wrapped her arms around him in a hug that felt like a mother's embrace—what he could remember of the ways of mothers. And all he wanted was to bury his head in her kindness and go far away from the memories, from the sight of Phil hooked up to machines. But he knew he had to be a man. He had to be the brother—the big brother—to Phil.

Peter buried his soiled, tired face into Ramona's shoulder, feeling her imbue him with a courage he was not sure he felt. Finally, he pulled away, his eyes wet.

Her own dark eyes were moist. "What happened to Phil? Is he OK?"

Peter brushed dirt from her jacket and shook his head. "He crashed his bike. Swelling of the brain... I don't know... they aren't really telling me much. Just that he is in a coma."

"My poor Phil. What can I do, my boy... my boys?" She smiled wanly at him.

"The doctor said there's nothing more to do right now. He's stable and heavily sedated. The nurse told me I can't even give blood right now." He glanced down again at the blood smears on his bike shorts.

She warmly stroked his arm. "Peter, everything will be all right. I *know* it will. Sometimes you have to trust in the angels."

"I hope so." Angels were Phil's department, not his. He remembered the first Christmas Eve after their parents died. Phil went with Ramona to the Catholic cathedral she always went to for midnight mass. Peter stayed home.

He blinked, shaking the memory from his brain.

"Don't worry, *mijo*." Ramona soothed. "I'll take care of everything at work. You… you take care of Phil."

Peter sighed, closed his eyes and nodded. He could smell Ramona's orange blossom perfume, the scent of citrus that dominated his memories of her.

When he opened his eyes again, at the end of the corridor, rushing towards him, was Sam. She passed Ramona, who was already scrolling on her phone and speaking to whomever it is people spoke to in times of crises. Ramona and Sam exchanged worried glances. As she neared Peter, Sam picked up her pace and finally threw her arms around his neck. Her scent was earthy—a musky sandalwood.

Peter stood stiffly. If he hugged Sam back, he would lose it. And out of the corner of his eye, he could spy Kyle heading in their direction. The last thing he wanted was for Kyle to see him looking weak. Peter needed to be the one in control. The one who had all the answers.

"OK, Peter, I think it's time for you to go home." Sam stepped back and surveyed him. Her curly hair—which she usually styled in a bun for work—was loose and spiraling down her back. She wore a loose batik-print spaghetti-strap dress and flip-flops instead of her usual black dress pants and silk blouse. He almost didn't recognize her—but for the dimple when she smiled. He even noticed her freckles were out in full force instead of hidden under foundation.

"Can't go home. Not yet."

She raised one eyebrow. "I have to tell you, I don't know that in the last four years or so that I've ever seen you looking so shitty. You need a shower, fresh clothes, and my guess is a meal."

He shook his head. "Please... Sam... take Kyle to his mom's. She'll be pissed I have him here so late."

Sam rolled her eyes. "Really? When I called her she immediately said she'd fry up some of her world-famous eggplant parm and leave it in a casserole dish on your doorstep. Heat at 350 for thirty minutes. She didn't sound the slightest bit pissed. In fact, she said, and I quote, 'Phil was one of the most very precious things about being married to Peter—along with Ramona.'"

Peter's eyes widened. That made no sense. Sarah hated being married to him. They fought about everything from vacations to what kind of sneakers Kyle wore.

"Look, Peter," Sam lowered her voice. "You might be surprised about some humans. If you give them a chance."

Peter turned away. He didn't want her to see his eyes. Then he faced Kyle.

"Stay at your mom's tonight. I'll pick you up from school on Monday. Try to work on that paper. And try not to worry about Uncle Phil. He'll pull through. I just know it."

"You can't promise that, Dad." Kyle scowled at him. "You, of all people, should know that."

Peter had always shielded his son from the story of his and Phil's loss. He wondered if Phil or Sarah filled him with talk of the tragedy. Why he no longer believed in the promises that fathers the world over made when times were scary. Peter said, "Fine. But look, we have to hold onto hope."

Kyle nodded. Sam gave Peter a reassuring look, threw her arm around Kyle's shoulders, and led him out of the hospital.

Peter glanced down at his bike gear. He had a gym bag in his car, and he was sure there was a pair of sweats and a sweatshirt in there. He walked down the corridor and into the night air.

He found the Tesla and opened the driver's-side door and sat behind the wheel. The stars were out, and the wind was blowing. He stared up at the sky and tried to breathe—but found the old stone lodged there.

He could never explain it. No matter how happy a day—like the afternoon at precisely 3:42 when Kyle was born. Or before that, when Sarah had left the pregnancy stick indicator on the counter of the bathroom sink so he could see the "plus" sign. Or his wedding day. Or the day he signed the contract on his deal with the studio. No matter the day, no matter the joy, the weight was there. A stone had lodged itself right in the center of his sternum. It warned him—don't hope too much. Don't believe too much. In a moment, your life could be destroyed.

He saw—right there, in the sky, like a vision—his mother. In a blink, he was in the back seat of the car, his brother clutching his crayon picture and his thermos. His mother turned around to blow him and

Phil kisses. Then she said, "Let's sing a song." She started singing "Heart of Gold." A Neil Young classic. Their dad chimed in. And she was smiling—when the bright lights of the truck illuminated her face, rendering her skin pale in the brilliance. And then there was the shattering of glass—and the horrific sounds. Screams. Metal against metal. And life was destroyed. In an instant. Boom!

Peter shut his eyes. But it didn't quiet the visions. He stood at the bottom of a mountain trail and watched his brother sail over a wooden railing. Next, a cracked helmet. A crumpled bike. Blood.

Peter pulled off his white Lycra bike shirt. He felt so foolish now. Who cared what kind out special outfit he wore as he biked? He reached over to the back seat and pulled his gym bag over to the front, finding and putting on a sweatshirt. Still white, but at least no bloodstains. He glanced over at the floor of the passenger side and saw Phil's black backpack. He opened it, and unzipped the inner pocket. He felt around. It was there. Of course, it was.

His hand emerged with the Superman thermos.

He whispered into the silence, "I wish I could be your superhero, Keats."

He leaned his head on the steering wheel.

He was no one's superhero. Not Phil's.

Not Kyle's.

He shook his head. No magic, no trickery of a man of steel could change what happened.

❧

*Sam drove the car. I stared out the window.*

*"Penny for your thoughts, Kyle."*

*"You'd have to up the ante on that for inflation." I offered her a smirk.*

*"All right. How about a cheeseburger and fries for your thoughts?"*

*Only then did I realize how hungry I was. I stared out the window again. "Sounds good."*

*"Um. Nope. That's not how this works."*

*"How what works?"*

*"You know, the whole spill-your-guts thing."*

*I didn't know what to say. Sam is someone who just listens and finds the truth. I remember when I once hid that I was flunking math. She figured it out long before my dad did and got me a tutor. He never even found out that I had a tutor, this cool guy—the one who taught me about the Fibonacci sequence just for "fun." Soon I had an A-, and Dad was none the wiser.*

*"Worried about your Uncle Phil?"*

*I nodded slowly.*

*"And?"*

*"And what?"*

*"Something else. What is it?"*

*I shrugged.*

*"You worried about your dad?"*

*I glanced over at her. She saw it in my eyes.*

*"He'll be okay."*

*I exhaled into the empty space between us in the car.*

*"Come on, Kyle. It's me. The one who told you that divorce wasn't fun—but that it would be OK. That both your parents love you."*

*Finally I whispered. "I don't know. He and Uncle Phil argued today. If something happens… before they can make it right between them? I don't think Dad'd ever get over it."*

*She reached out and patted my arm. "People are more resilient than you think."*

*"Yeah, but my dad is the only person who thinks he can control the universe and everyone and everything in it. He once told me that was why he created movies."*

*"Why?"*

*"Because he could make sure the characters did what he wanted. They never disappointed him."*

*"But people aren't characters in the movies."*

"I know that."

"But you think your dad doesn't."

How could I tell her? His Fibonacci sequence, the one he had carefully controlled since he was a boy and his parents were killed, had just betrayed him. He thought he knew the sequence. He thought he knew which number came next.

1, 1, 2, 3, 5, 8, 13, 21…

But now the numbers were as unpredictable as… well, people.

And my dad would never understand that.

Perfection was a burden he thought he had to carry on his own.

# A Box of Memories

*don't have a brother. I always wanted one. Or a sister. I have a dog. At my mom's. My dad doesn't like when I bring my dog to his house. He says he tracks dog hair through the house and ruins its "sensibility." Like a house has… I don't know… feelings or something.*

*I named my dog Buddy—for Buddy Guy. And I love Buddy. A lot. And I think he understands me when I tell him my problems. Because if I tell him I am sad, his eyes get droopy. A dog has sensibilities.*

*A house is just drywall and beams.*

*I looked out at the stars from my bedroom window. Buddy was snoring gently on the end of my bed. Mom tells me to make him sleep on his dog bed. But, to me, that would make Buddy feel bad.*

*Anyway, I tried to imagine just how my dad was going to deal with all this. Once Buddy ate a shoe. One of my dad's Italian loafers, which Dad has told me 487 times was worth $900. And that's just for the left one Buddy ate (another reason Buddy isn't allowed at his house). And Buddy was sick, and I was torn up about it. The vet said we had to watch Buddy. To see if... well, it would pass. Otherwise, Buddy would need surgery. So if that's how I felt about Buddy eating a tasseled loafer, I couldn't imagine how my dad was going to deal with it if Uncle Phil didn't pull through.*

*Uncle Phil was in a coma. In a place where we couldn't reach him. Where we just had to watch him. And my dad couldn't do much about it.*

*Patience, by the way, has never been my dad's thing.*

Peter had watched as the families of other patients in the ICU went home for the night. He wasn't going to leave his brother.

"Come on, Phil... I know you're in there."

Peter blinked back tears, then tried again. "Come onnnn, Keats. It's me..." He put his head in his hands. The words stung in his throat. "It's me. Coleridge."

76

The male nurse from earlier appeared in the darkened doorway.

"Can he hear me?" Peter asked.

"We like to think so... though no one has ever come out of a coma since I've been here and been able to tell us what they've heard. I like to think they hear the emotions in your words. I don't know if they can really hear what you are saying. Hear the words."

Peter looked at the nurse, nodded, then looked back at Phil.

"You never did hear what I was saying Phil," he whispered.

Peter blinked. The machines. The hospital smell. The white sheets. It was like the memory of long ago. He stood and walked over to the lone window to outside. He moved the slats on the blinds. A view of the parking lot. In the dark of the glass, he saw his own face, cast in shadows. It was like seeing himself through the looking glass.

Young Peter screaming silently, tears running down dark shadows on his pink cheeks.

Peter saw shimmers of broken glass in this hospital parking lot. But then, in the looking glass, he saw a thousand specks of glass on the pavement, catching moonlight and siren light in odd formations.

An ambulance pulled up to the emergency room bay, and three paramedics pulled out a person on a stretcher. In the looking glass, Peter saw young Phil getting strapped to a stretcher.

Peter wiped at his face. Where had all these tears come from? He hadn't even cried at their parents' funeral, while Phil had buried his head in Ramona's lap and sobbed.

Peter stared into the looking glass one more time. Then he walked over to Phil's bedside. He leaned over, and put his mouth right at Phil's ear. In his most pleading voice, he whispered, "Fight this, Keats. Come back to me. Please."

Leaving the hospital, he climbed into his Tesla and drove off into the night.

Peter spent most of the next day visiting his brother. It was a quiet Sunday, and there was absolutely no change in Phil's condition. Later that night, after Peter returned home again, sleep eluded him. When his iPhone alarm went off Monday morning, Peter showered but forgot to shave. He misplaced his watch and forgot to put gel in his hair. Driving to the studio, he kept glancing at Phil's Superman thermos in the passenger seat and talking to it, like it was somehow Phil.

"Come on, Bro. You need to pull out of this."

Disheveled, clearly short on sleep, he strolled into his office ignoring most of his employees, who whispered amongst themselves. He glared at them. The rumor mill was obviously working overtime.

At the morning's big meeting, he stood before a group of his creative team and aimed a pointer at a series of storyboards lined up on a row of easels.

Voice a little hoarse, he said, "Do you see? A story can't *progress* without *resistance*. We need an inciting incident and antagonistic forces—villains, nature, bad luck—to create conflict and drama."

He looked out on their eager faces. They were all film school graduates. They *knew* this stuff. But somehow, lately, he sensed that they—he and his entire team—were missing something very important. He stood there, with the pointer in his hand, as if in suspended animation.

He turned to face the easels, still not sure of his next point, when Sam popped her head in the door.

"Peter?"

Peter looked up. "Where was I?"

Sam said, more insistently, "Peter!"

"What?!"

Sam mimed answering the phone. She silently mouthed, "Hospital."

Peter nodded. He looked at his team. "That's it for now. Take a fresh look at it. And really try to *feel* it this time."

An hour later, Peter sat opposite Dr. Arjun Singh in a room overflowing with medical texts, and a tidy wooden desk with a bonsai tree on the corner. Dr. Singh wore a blue turban that matched the shade of blue of his silk tie. His eyes were warm, and he spoke carefully, seemingly choosing each word with deliberation.

"The good news is we tapered some of the medications, and your brother has emerged from his coma."

Peter softly tapped the desk corner near his chair and exhaled, hugely relieved. "Terrific. When can he go home?"

"Well, there is a bit more to this. The... less good news is that he's suffering from retrograde amnesia."

Peter shook his head and sighed. "He doesn't know what happened? That he was in an accident?"

Dr. Singh's drew his mouth into a thin line. "It is actually more complicated than just not remembering the accident. He doesn't... know his name. Doesn't know what year it is. It's very likely he might not know who you are, so I don't want you to be alarmed."

"Alarmed? I'd say it's pretty god-damned alarming that my only brother doesn't know who he is."

Dr. Singh nodded. "I understand. But I want you to know that in most cases this is temporary. But unfortunately, we will not know for certain until some weeks from now."

"Weeks?! How *many* weeks?"

"I'm sorry. I'm not sure. We are on the brain's timetable. More specifically, Philip's brain's timetable. He has had a terrible accident. There was brain swelling. It is difficult to say."

"OK, Doc. Look, I am not going to hold you to anything. But what does the data say?"

Dr. Singh's voice was calm. "The data varies."

"It varies. OK, what percent of patients snap out of it? Does that vary, too? Is my brother going to be a babbling idiot for the rest of his life?"

"He is not a babbling idiot now. He has amnesia."

"Fine. What does the data show for people regaining their memories?"

"I'm afraid it varies. And to tell you anything different to make you feel better would be dishonest."

Peter tried to contain himself. He said his words evenly, trying not to reveal the anger he was feeling. "So... you're telling me my brother's back but not *really*."

"That's one way of putting it. But let us remain hopeful. It is early days yet..." He paused. "Please, bring in some personal items: photographs, memorabilia, an iPod playlist. Anything that might help jog his memory. Do you know what kind of music he likes?"

Peter shifted in his seat. "I'll... uhh... bring in some photos."

Peter went to visit his brother, who was being moved to a regular room three flights down, but when he got there, he was told Phil was having an MRI and wouldn't be back for at least two hours.

Instead, Peter went in search of some things from Phil's place to bring him back to reality.

⌒

Peter hopped in his Tesla and headed to the rundown, concrete motel on the corner of a busy intersection that housed his brother's studio apartment. And he used the word "apartment" loosely. Peter walked past rows of closed doors and fished around for Phil's room key, finding it in his left suit pocket.

Peter did his best to step around discarded trash on the second-story landing. He finally arrived at Phil's door, which was cracked open. Peter double-checked the room number. *Yeah, this is the dump.* He warily pushed the door open, stepped in, and removed his Ray-Bans.

Peter jumped. *WTF?!*

Cross-armed, staring straight at Peter was a fat, hairy, balding man in a filthy white tank top.

"Who the hell are you?" the man snarled.

"What?!… Who the hell are *you*?"

"I'm the soupa… What are *you* doin' here, Mr. Fancy Suit? The stiff owe you money, too?"

"Look, the 'stiff's' my brother. And he's been in an accident. I'm here to pick up a few of his things. He's in the hospital."

"Jeez. I'm sorry. Sure, go ahead, pick up some stuff. But before you do——"

Peter raised one eyebrow. "Yeah?"

"You got my rent?"

Peter resisted the urge to roll his eyes. Everybody had an angle. He nonchalantly removed his billfold from his inside breast pocket and slid out his black American Express card. Holding it between his index finger and middle finger, he gestured it toward the sweaty, hairy Philistine.

"Just ring up what he owes you."

"Ring up?! Where d' ya think ya are, Barneys?" He sneered and brushed Peter's hand away. Then he walked by toward the open front door.

"Look, have the cash here by the end of the week or this used bookstore goes out to the curb. Got it?" He slammed the door behind him.

Peter stood fuming. *What an asshole.* He put the Amex card back.

Exhaling, Peter warily began poking through cabinets and drawers, stepping around books. He had thought the super's comment about a used bookstore was weird. But now he realized there were piles of books everywhere.

He reached out and casually picked up a book from a tall stack. He opened it at a bookmark and read aloud, finding his voice tight.

*Very little grows on jagged rock.*
*Be ground.*
*Be crumbled, so wildflowers will*
*come up where you are.*

He paused, then shook his head. *Poor Phil.* He looked around. The studio was so dimly lit. He looked closer at the walls and realized they were a dull industrial grey—and definitely in need of a new coat of paint. He returned the book to the pile and opened Phil's closet door. A few pairs of hanging khaki pants—all wrinkled. Like why bother hanging them. Next to them were T-shirts—one black T-shirt bore a quote by Keats. Peter slid the T-shirts across the hanger bar. Another black T with a quote by Byron. Man, his brother was hung up on old poets.

The next were all rock T-shirts. Some were from concerts Phil, by the looks of the T-shirts and tour names, attended over two decades ago.

Peter looked around. It was a weird feeling, almost like he was spying on his brother. They were so different. How much did he really know about Phil? More books stood like towers on the floor.

Peter looked up and saw a somewhat battered cardboard filing box on the shelf. On the side, written in sloppy black Sharpie, was the word "memories." Peter easily reached the box, chuckling to himself. Phil probably had to stand on tiptoe to grasp it. Peter pulled it down, then plopped on Phil's unmade bed. He laughed to himself about that, too. He and Kyle slept on two-thousand-thread-count Egyptian cotton sheets. Phil's sheets, he mused, were so faded they *may* have been left over from Phil's college days.

Peter opened the box and removed the first two old "memories:" high school photos. Phil was dressed in a Neil Young T-shirt, his hair long and unkempt. His lopsided smile, and big blue eyes projecting humor. Phil always looked like he was thinking about an inside joke.

Peter half-smiled. The next photo was Peter grinning, in sports coat and tie. A very wide tie. *What the hell am I smiling about?*

He dropped the photos on the bed and looked in the box for the next memory. It was "the" Neil Young T-shirt. Peter shook his head, held it up, examined it. Tossed it on the bed. His brother was obsessed—utterly obsessed by Young.

Peter reached back into the box. An incredulous look passed over his face. *What's this?! This is from... before.*

It was a photo of teenaged Peter standing next to six-year-old Phil. His little brother sat wide-eyed on his first "real" bike—metallic green, banana seat, "sissy bar."

Peter stared at the photo and smiled, remembering... life before.

He shut his eyes. He could picture it. They had a typical, early 1970s family living room—complete with orange velour chairs, and a couch with yellow flowers. Their kitchen had lime-green appliances. Their downstairs bathroom looked like someone vomited Pepto-Bismol on the tiles. Even their toilet was pink.

Peter laughed to himself. No wonder he liked everything white and clean now, no velour in sight.

The day of the bicycle picture, their entire house had buzzed with friends and neighbors and a few of their parents' older relatives. Cute, shy Phil had been in the center of the to-do. Paint on his face, drawing in his hand, he grinned in every picture Peter had in his mind. It was as if he were watching an old VHS tape, or and even older Super-8 film. Each frame was a flash of a memory, preserved in his mind, like a fly in amber.

He was *there* again, through some time-travel of the inner mind.

Adults were fawning over Phil, who looked a little uncomfortable. Someone pinched Phil's cheek. "He's so cute!" the woman fawned.

Peter, meanwhile, sat stiff-backed on their yellow-flowered couch between two great-aunties, Dixie plates of food on their laps. Peter looked at the buffet table, laden with what would now be considered vintage Tupperware, and dishes like layered Jell-O molds and ambrosia salad—Phil's favorite with tiny little marshmallows.

He exchanged glances with Phil. His little brother's eyes widened in a look of sheer panic. He was overwhelmed with all the attention. Peter put his plate down on their Lucite coffee table, ran over, grabbed Phil's tiny hand in his own, and swept him out of the room.

In a quiet hallway, right outside their parents' bedroom, Peter knelt down to Phil's height. He looked right into his eyes. "It's OK, Phil. It's a lot of commotion to be the birthday boy." He smiled at his brother. "Here's what we'll do. If you don't want to be someplace, you give me a secret sign, and I'll come get you, OK?"

"What kind of sign?" Phil asked.

"How 'bout this?" Peter grinned and stuck his own index finger in his ear. "Put your finger in your ear like this and wiggle it, OK? Like you have an itchy ear."

Phil laughed and mimicked his brother. "Like this?"

"Yup, little buddy. Just like that! It'll be our secret sign."

A siren sounded in the distance, in the now, followed by the heavy bass of a car playing some very loud music. The noise brought Peter out of his reverie. He smiled and lightly placed the photo on the bed. Reaching into the box, he pulled out a colorful crayon drawing. Peter squinted down at it and felt a chill trickle down his spine. His eyes widened. *Oh my God!*

The memory pulled him beneath the waves of grief like an undertow. He felt like he was in a trance. Phil was next to him in the backseat of their parents' car. Phil was coloring furiously—creating that very same crayon drawing. He was totally engaged—the way he did everything from riding his banana-seat bike to coloring to feeding his hamster.

Peter looked at his brother's drawing. His eyes lit up with pride. He had told his mom that Phil was going to be an artist someday.

 He smiled at the artistry of his little brother, gave Phil a big hug and started telling him a fantastical story. *"Su arte va cambiar el mundo!"*

Their dad, in the front seat, glanced at their mom in the passenger seat. "What'd he say?"

"Ramona's teaching them Spanish. Our little guys will be bilingual!"

She turned and smiled at them, blowing them each kisses. "Let's sing a song."

And there it was in slow motion again. Their mother starting to sing in her off-key, happy way, then she turned to face the front, and in that moment, the lights from the oncoming truck illuminated her face, pale like a porcelain doll.

And then it all froze. The fly in amber, the agony preserved forever.

His mother's face registered horror.

His father stuck his arm out to the side, as if to protect her.

Phil's Superman thermos twirled across the back seat as if thrown, pirouetting like a dancer.

Peter felt a single bead of sweat trace down his cheek—or was it a tear. In another blink he saw himself and Phil in matching black suits. Each of them had a dark tie—Phil's was a clip-on. They each had fresh haircuts, their hair parted neatly and slicked back.

Ramona—young, her hair halfway down her back, tied with a black velvet ribbon—held each of their hands. Peter was already slightly taller than her small frame. But Phil looked so small next to her. She squeezed their hands and whispered, "It is OK, my boys. We will do this together."

She walked them, slowly, to the open grave. Two coffins were side by side. On a table were dozens of pink peonies—their mother's favorite flower—their stems clipped, leaves removed so each was a solitary burst of bloom and color.

Ramona let go of their hands. She nodded—almost imperceptibly. She walked, head tilted upwards, as if to keep the tears gathering in her eyes from escaping. She picked up a pink peony, then kissed it. She walked over to the open gravesite, and tossed the flower in the grave.

Peter was next. He swallowed, and tried to concentrate on Ramona and Phil. He did exactly as she had done. He walked to the table, chose a deeper-shaded peony, kissed it, walked to the gravesite and tossed it in.

He approached Phil and leaned down. He whispered, "Your turn."

Phil, rather than walking to the table of peonies, put his finger in his ear and wiggled it around. He looked up at his brother imploringly.

Peter felt all the eyes of the mourners on him, on them. "I know, buddy." He leaned down on one knee, unconcerned that he was soiling the pant leg of his brand-new suit.

"You can do this."

Phil shook his head. In his free hand he held his Superman thermos. He clutched it to his chest and snuggled it like a teddy bear. "Let's go home, Petey."

Peter nodded and looked up at Ramona. She gave a short nod. Peter stood and looked up at the sky. Home would never be home again. Not really.

Peter looked down at the drawing again. Hands shaking, he slowly placed the cover on the box and sat quietly with it on his lap.

If Phil lost his memories, what did that mean? Did any of it really even happen? If Phil had amnesia, then he alone was the only one who remembered the way their mother made gingerbread men in December, and the way their dad took them to fly kites on windy spring days. And the horrible night, all of that went away. And four became two.

⚬

*I have a box.*

*Just like Uncle Phil, I collected some memories. I have a blue ribbon in there from a science fair experiment involving a volcano that actually ended with Mom having to repaint the dining room.*

I have a picture I stole out of my parents' wedding album of the two of them looking crazy in love. I know they aren't going to get back together.

"He's too controlling," Mom would say.

"She's so difficult," he would say.

But every kid likes to think he was conceived in love. Not like "conceived." Gross. But you know, born into a family where two people love each other a lot. So I have that picture.

I have a picture of my dad and Uncle Phil when they were boys. My dad doesn't even know I have it. Mom gave it to me. She actually sort of threw it at me. See, one time my dad was just being really... um, "Peter-ish" (which is what my mom calls it; Uncle Phil and I would joke it was a "Coleridge Moment"). He was giving me a hard time about hitting the books when I was at his house and so when I was home with Mom, I was complaining. And she ran to her desk and pulled out the picture, and she shoved it toward me.

"This," she jabbed her finger at the picture, "was probably the last time your dad wasn't so Peter-ish. Somehow, this little kid here, he disappeared and we all got stuck with... Peter. He's not a bad guy. But..." She suddenly smiled and messed up my hair. "Preaching to the

*choir. Look, know this. Your dad loves you. And so do I."*
*She winked at me.*

*So my box. Yeah. I have all that. And I have the cat collar from Angel, who died of feline leukemia when I was ten. I have some rocks that apparently I thought were cool when I was like five years old. And I have an arrowhead—a real one—I found in Maine when I went to summer camp.*

*But in a lot of ways, I don't need the box.*

*I have playlists.*

*Now, I will admit, when I make a playlist, it's fairly easy technologically. I don't have to go find fifty different vinyl albums, queue up songs, and then tape them. Apparently, this is the way they did this way back when.*

*Um. No. For me, I just find songs I like, and I pop them onto their assigned lists by pressing a button.*

*I make a new playlist every month. On it are the songs that are the soundtrack for my life that particular month. So, the month that I found out Tori had decided to go to Homecoming with that Eric guy? When every single guy and girl in the entire school knew he was a total tool and was just gonna break her heart. Well, my playlist consisted of Corrinne Bailey Ray, Etta, and that ultimate heartbreak song: "Last Goodbye" by Jeff Buckley.*

*Because, you know, it's even sadder because the dude died way too young.*

*Anyway, I think that Uncle Phil… he had a soundtrack of Neil Young. He heard it. Even if it wasn't playing at that moment. It's like when I have to do something I don't want to—like clean the garage, I'll put on headphones. But once, my old headphones broke, so I hummed my soundtrack. And whether it was playing out loud, or in my head, it was still my soundtrack.*

*But Dad didn't have that. I think I know why.*

*Just a theory.*

*All his movies have soundtracks. And he hires the best composers in the business. But a movie soundtrack is all about one thing for Dad: what it can do for him… to manipulate people's feelings to match what is going on up there on the screen. Or, you know, to have a singing toaster or a singing mermaid or whatever sell stuffed animals and Happy Meals.*

*Uncle Phil told me about a quote from Victor Hugo: "Music expresses that which cannot be said and on which it is impossible to be silent."*

*Dad doesn't feel the soundtrack the way me and Uncle Phil do. It's just different. Dudes with soundtracks feel it in their heart, blues guys feel it in their veins. It is an expression of things unsaid. But for my dad and people like him, they feel music in their heads. It never crosses the threshold to their soul.*

# Blank Slate

*inyl.*

*There's something about that hiss.*

*That sense that someone recorded this album in a studio, pouring their dreams into this session, and then it was pressed. And now you get to be in that sound booth, listening to it just like the guy producing the record, and it just takes you back. Which is silly because, frankly, it takes you back to before I was even born. But something about it.*

*Don't get me wrong: I've got everything digital and downloaded and on a cloud.*

*But then I heard vinyl in this old used record store. And I was hooked. My mother had this old stereo in a box in the attic. I bought a few vinyls of old blues, and I would lie down on my bed and listen, hearing every imperfect hiss, slight scratch, just this sense that the music was bigger than I was, and it was filling my room from across time.*

*Now, my dad always told me vinyl was stupid. I mean, why have that hiss if you can have something "pristine"? Crystal clear.*

*Clarity is a word Dad liked a lot. Clarity.*

*So I found this old vinyl LP of Django Reinhardt. And on it, apparently recorded in a café in Paris or something, you hear him calling out in French over the music. Now Reinhardt is an interesting guy. He was a Romani guitarist, who was severely burned in a fire. Two of his fingers were disfigured, and he had to re-learn how to play guitar with only eight fingers. Anyway, I listened—and listened—and listened to that vinyl album and those songs over and over. And I loved that I could hear Django— from beyond the grave—just jamming. Now, my dad muttered something about the background noise, the shout in French over the music, as ruining it.*

*"You can get the music of Django digitally remastered," he told me.*

*But I don't want it digitally remastered.*

*To me, the sounds on that old vinyl are the sounds of musicians so into the moment and the music that they transcend time. They created something that can't be re-*

*created again. You can digitally remaster it all you want, but you'll never digitally remaster the energy in that café.*

*Now, Dad, as all this stuff was going on with Uncle Phil, was in the midst of a work crisis. His studio was making a movie with a talking, singing toaster—which was supposed to be a lot cuter than it sounds. And what Dad couldn't pull from any of his team was energy. Maybe it was because he had too much clarity.*

*I know that sounds a little crazy. But if you want energy, you have to expect a little chaos.*

Peter dropped his briefcase on his desk with a sigh. He opened the butter-soft leather case and gently removed Phil's crayon drawing. He pinned it to his bulletin board. There was no change in Phil. The MRI hadn't shown a blood clot or a tumor or even residual swelling in the brain, nothing neurological that the doctors could point to and explain the amnesia.

Peter faced his windows, his silhouette a greyish reflection against the glass. *What must it be like to look in the mirror and not even recognize the face staring back at you?*

Peter shook his head. He didn't want to think about it. He didn't want to imagine Phil being trapped in his own mind, forever. Sure, they fought. But wasn't that what *brothers* did? Now, it was as if their whole relationship, all their history, was gone. As if it never happened.

He had driven back to the hospital the previous night, and he and Dr. Singh had entered Phil's room.

Dr. Singh began, gingerly. "Mr. Anderson, there is someone here to see you."

Phil, pale against the while hospital sheets, looked up at Peter and Dr. Singh. "Yes? Another doctor?"

Peter turned his head so neither of them could see the tears in his eyes. He exhaled loudly, then faced his brother.

"No, Phil. I'm your brother, Peter."

Phil stared at him. "Wow. Like… I feel like I should know you. But I don't."

Dr. Singh walked closer to the bedside. He patted Phil's leg. "Feeling like you *should* is a good sign. That means on a subconscious level you recognize something familiar about your brother. That is very good."

"But Doc," Phil said, "shouldn't I be better by now?"

"You had a severe blow to your head. You must give it time."

Peter walked closer. "Can you remember anything from... the accident?"

"Nope."

"What about childhood? Remember Honi?"

"Honey? Did I like honey?"

"No. Our dog. The best damn dog in the whole world. You picked her out of the litter."

Phil stared at him blankly. "I wish I did. Sounds like a great dog."

Dr. Singh smiled down at Phil. "One day, I am confident, you will recover these memories. We're going to let you rest now."

He gently led Peter from the room. In the hallway, after the door to Phil's room was shut, Peter began pacing.

"My own brother doesn't remember me. Listen... our parents died when we were little kids. We're all... we're all each other has. I have a son, but... Phil's got nobody but *me*. So you tell me: *When* is my brother going to remember the greatest dog in the world." He swallowed. "And me?"

"We cannot be certain. The mysteries of the human brain are not always predictable. But I do feel confident. He needs time."

Peter stared down at his Rolex. Time. What the hell? How much? He was used to getting things done. And mysteries and uncertainties were definitely not in his plans.

He wanted his brother back.

Now.

In his office, Peter peered down at his Rolex. Time to get ready for the meeting. With one last glance at the crayon drawing, he headed toward the conference room.

He walked in—the table was long and gleaming, mahogany wood, polished to a sheen. On the far wall a large flat screen TV was mounted, and a side buffet table was being fussed over by Sam. She arranged a platter of bagels, and a large silver tub containing ice and bottled waters. A tall silver urn contained coffee, its aroma filled the room.

Peter stood at the head of the conference room table leafing through documents. His eyes drooped from lack of sleep. He had tossed and turned about Phil all damn night.

Ramona sat to his left, like the queen at a banquet. In front of her sat a delicate teacup and saucer, and she dunked her herbal tea—a jasmine creation imported from Morocco—in hot water.

Zack Wells strode in. In his mid-thirties, the comedic actor and "voice" of Oscar the toaster always seemed a living embodiment of the characters he portrayed. He wore a bright Hawaiian-print shirt, cargo shorts, and flip-flops, his shaggy hair clearly still damp from his morning shower. He flipped his Ray Bans up on top of his head.

Peter looked at Zack. Despite taking countless meetings at the studio, the guy always ignored the dress code. Unspoken, but still. Everyone else dressed the part.

"Hey Zack, you're a bit... early."

"Sorry, Pete," he grinned, a deep dimple in his right cheek, a twinkle to his blue eyes. He made a dramatic bow toward Ramona. "Good morning, Ramona. You look lovely today."

Ramona smiled in her best Mona Lisa way, enigmatic and regal.

Sam finished laying out napkins and small plates. She smiled at him, part smirk. "Hey, Zackster."

"Hey, Sammy. Nice bagels, baby."

Peter didn't need all this chit-chat now. Not when he was prepping for the meeting. Sam and Ramona knew him well enough to not make small talk when he was getting ready to speak.

He cleared his throat. "Yeah... Zack? I know you've got a lot on your mind, but please try to remember... it's Peter, not Pete."

"Sorry, Pete."

Peter shook his head. Sam raised one eyebrow and hurried over to steer Zack to an open seat at the *far* end of the conference table.

About ten minutes later, employees began filing in. They carried mugs of coffee, listlessly flopping into seats, or moving to the bagels, grabbing breakfast, and then sitting and eating quietly. Some carried storyboards. Most were silent.

"It's Zack!" a woman from animation said.

At that, Zack launched into several of his cartoon voices, making everyone smile at his shtick. He was like a stand-up comic, loosening up the crowd. Everyone was soon laughing—except Peter. He was preoccupied with papers in his hands.

Finally, Peter straightened up, steely-eyed. Time to get things going, time to *fix* this damn movie.

"OK let's get to it. Kelly, jump right in and explain that scene with Oscar and Stanley."

Kelly, one of his creative team, with electric blue hair and multiple piercings—but dressed professionally—straightened up. As she got ready to speak, the conference door swung open.

A frazzled young woman entered. Juggling documents, balancing her coffee, she slunk down to the far end of the table and scooted into an empty chair.

Peter glared. In fact, his glare followed her all the way to her seat. *What the hell's wrong with people today?* After she sat, she arranged her papers on the table in front of her before finally realizing Peter was staring at her. She froze, put her hands in her lap, and appeared to want to become invisible.

Peter turned back to Kelly. "Go ahead, Kelly."

"Yes... Mr. Anderson." Suddenly, struck by the sea of faces staring at her, she looked flustered. "So my idea is... so Oscar's being harassed by Stanley, right? So Stanley takes Oscar's cord, while he's sleeping, and he ties it around the oven handle." She smiled. "That's pretty funny, right? Clever on Stanley's part."

Zack looked at her, confused. But everyone else gazed at her expectantly.

"Anyway, so when Oscar wakes up he realizes this, so... he becomes enraged, right? He turns bright red, and pops burnt toast out of his head, which..." She stammered. "So anyway... remember what Pixar did with *Inside Out*? How they showed—"

Peter held up both his hands. "OK, stop right there."

Everyone around the table froze.

"First off... fuck Pixar! OK?!"

Everyone squirmed. Even Ramona's eyes widened a little. Peter was known for never cursing in the office. But damn, he was frustrated.

He narrowed his eyes at Zack, who choked on his bagel, trying not to laugh.

"Look, Kelly... I know how good you are. But you know better than to have Oscar do *that*. It goes completely against one of the most important principles of story development. Tell me... what's vitally important with regards to characters, besides the fact that they drive the story?"

Kelly's cheeks flushed. "That they stay true to who they are?"

"Exactly! That they stay true to who they *were*... who they've *been*... their backstory." He pointed at his chest. "What's inside of them."

He looked around the table intently—avoiding Zack—but focusing on his creative team. "Think about it. All of a sudden Oscar's going to change who he is, who the audience *thinks* he is, and become... what? A small-minded little shit?"

Kelly furrowed her brow. "I get what you're saying, but we don't want him to be dull, right?"

"Do we want the characters to be complex, interesting? Of course, we do. Just like we want the scenes to be interesting. But it has to be consistent... coherent. We want people to *believe*. Right?

Peter looked around, assessing. Then he continued.

"Look... is Superman dull?"

Kelly raised her pierced eyebrow. "I wouldn't go out with him. I mean, the red boots? Really?"

She looked around for approval. Zack offered her a thumbs-up, cream cheese on the corners of his mouth.

Peter gave her an exasperated look. "OK, yes, the red boots are a turn-off, Kelly. I wouldn't go out with him either. But what if the writers created a scene where mild-mannered Clark Kent became a vulgar womanizer. It would confuse the audience. Cause them to question the story. Knock them out of their—"

Peter extended his arms, palms up, nodding. His team knew the cue.

Everyone, in sing-song voice and in unison chorused, "Suspension of disbelief." Except Zack, who was looking around, trying to mouth along through cheeks stuffed with half-chewed bagel.

"Sus... pen... ders?"

Peter glanced over at Zack and raised his eyebrows. Zack raised his eyebrows in return. *Oh yeah, this is going well,* Peter thought.

"You all know the fundamentals of storytelling. So let's back up again to what Kelly was suggesting. And in fact, let's go deeper. Who is our little toaster, Oscar?"

Blank stares and silence were all he got from the room. Peter felt his frustration rising.

"Oscar is Winnie the *fucking* Pooh! Would Winnie the Pooh get—" He lifted his hands and made air quotes. "—pissed off?!"

Zack swallowed his food and swigged some water. "Well… Winnie the *fucking* Pooh might."

Zack grinned and looked around the room. Everyone wanted to laugh, judging by their eyes, but their faces were pressed into frozen expressions. They didn't dare even smile.

Peter let Zack's comment pass. "This is storytelling 101 people. When someone watches a movie, they want to get lost in the story. But, the moment you throw in a left hook like that, it'll break their immersion and snap them—" He snapped his fingers. "Right back to reality."

The woman who had arrived late raised her hand slightly, and asked, "So Mr. Anderson? We have to make the characters more… real?"

Peter sighed. "There's nothing *real* about what we create. But… we must make them 'believable.' Which means their behaviors must make sense."

He walked over to a large easel. Several pictures of characters were drawn in black marker. He gestured to the image of angry Oscar.

"Now, if we *want* Oscar to get angry... to act different from how the audience expects, we need to explain it. Because no one will accept that a character can have such a schizophrenic personality, unless he's eccentric or has... lost his memory or something."

Peter exhaled and for a moment, his body was there, but his mind wasn't. He was frozen in thought. Then, it was as if he saw the characters coming to life on the easel.

He saw Oscar falling off a counter, landing on his toaster head. Clang! Seeing cartoon stars, looking lost, confused. Oscar has lost his memory.

Just like Phil.

Peter stood mouth agape. His employees' eyes frantically darted around the room. No one seemed to know whether they should say something, or let the awkward silence go on.

Finally, Ramona took the lead. She stood, smoothed her skirt, and said, "That's it for today. Get back to your storyboards, and we'll reconvene tomorrow morning."

Employees scooped up their documents, quickly filing out past a motionless Peter, casting furtive glances in his direction.

Sam rushed to Zack and put her hands on his shoulders to hurry him out before he could say anything. "Come on," she whispered. "He clearly needs a moment."

Zack rose, started to leave then stopped. He turned back to face Peter.

Sam held her breath. Zack looked at Peter, then smoothly reached around him to the food tray. He scooped up a few bagels, placing one between his teeth and the other in his pants pocket, and strode out of the conference room.

Ramona guided Peter to his office. She sat him down on his leather couch. She took the wingback opposite him, tapping her foot nervously. This was so unlike her Peter. After a few minutes, Sam walked in, her face registering stress.

"Sam, please sit down," Peter said softly. He was emerging from whatever fugue state he had entered.

Sam sat in a leather wingback chair. "What's going on? Is there something you aren't telling us about Phil?"

"He's the same. I saw him last night. No change. None. He doesn't even know who I am." He pursed his lips. "Listen, I want to run something by both of you. It's a bit… unorthodox. And I'm going to need your help."

Both women murmured, "Of course."

Peter looked at Sam. "You paint, right? You're a trained artist?"

"I'm shocked you remember." She smiled. "I studied at University. I still dabble a bit. Oils, mostly——"

"Great." He cut her off. "So today in our meeting, something came to me." He stood and walked over to the bulletin board. He gingerly unpinned Phil's crayon drawing. "Phil has no memories."

Ramona looked at him, puzzled. "We know, Peter."

"So what if we created *new* ones for him?"

⤳

*So you ever wonder how it was that Jimi Hendrix decided to play the Star-Spangled Banner like some electric acid rock masterpiece? Was he a genius? Or crazy? Or are geniuses always a little of both?*

*Maybe the genius is just someone who has been brought to the edge, brought to their knees—and now doesn't care what anyone thinks.*

*So with what follows, my dad is either crazy. Or a genius.*

*Or just a grieving brother with nothing left to lose.*

# The Man with the Plan

*ature or nurture?*

*Hard work or talent?*

*People see my dad on magazine covers and stuff, and assume he is a creative genius. My mom actually told me his IQ one time. Yep. Genius.*

*But he would tell anyone who listens that discipline and dedication and hard work—relentless hard work— got him where he is today. He discounts the creativity. Creativity—to Peter Anderson—is something that can be managed. When people interview with him, he tells them that if they want a nine-to-five job, a job where there's the whole "work-life" balance thing, they've come to the wrong studio. I mean, he does nice things for his people. They get great bonuses. Once, when this lady in accounting's husband got terminal cancer, Dad literally paid for them to take a cruise to Alaska—first class all the way—before the guy died. And he did it in secret, too. Sam told me. He didn't want anyone else to know.*

*But if a project is late, or if the team is on a roll, they'll all stay past midnight. That's another reason my parents got divorced. He was never home.*

*So now my dad had this idea that all he needed to do was give Uncle Phil a life. Not the life he had. A new life. With new memories.*

*What my dad kind of didn't realize was that he was creating Uncle Phil in my dad's image. He was going to make him believe a different story about himself, a story of success on my dad's terms.*

*All I will say is my dad's heart was in the right place.*

*But, ever notice that when someone says "his heart was in the right place" it's usually because they have colossally screwed up?*

*Yeah.*

The loft was incredible. Light streamed in from every floor-to-ceiling window. Industrial piping ran overhead. Natural brick covered the walls.

Ramona stood, arms crossed, looking it over.

Shoes clapped on the hardwood floor behind her. Ramona wheeled around and smiled. Sam stood at the entrance, holding a large trash bag.

"Hi, Sam. C'mon in."

Sam surveyed the space. "So this is it. I mean, it's pretty impressive. Straight out of central casting. I suppose it's a good thing we both work in the Hollywood machinery?"

She set down the bag. "I can't believe I agreed to this."

Silence filled the loft.

Ramona nodded. "I know. I know. But maybe a new environment will help. Let's face it, how he was living wasn't."

She looked at Sam with eyes that displayed confidence, despite the concern that shrouded them. "I raised them. I should know."

"I suppose, but honestly Ramona… it just doesn't *feel* right to me. I mean, get Peter the latest profit projections. Check. Order bagels for the meeting. Check. Choose the locale for the Christmas party. Check. Line up a meeting with the latest investor or A-list actor. Got you covered, Peter. But this?"

"I know, but nothing we're doing can't be *undone*."

"I suppose."

"He can always go back to the life he was living. Let's trust Peter on this. His intentions are good. Deep down, my Peter has a good heart."

"And the road to hell *is* paved with…"

"Yes, I know."

Ramona cast a sidelong look at Sam and then offered a rueful smile. "I am going to have faith. And I suppose time will tell. So… what's in the bag?"

"It's a bunch of Phil's clothes. Peter wanted me to use them to size up his new wardrobe. He'll look a lot spiffier when I'm through with him."

Sam took a deep breath, making peace with her instincts. Finally, she gestured to a large drawing table.

"Was this Peter's place before he bought the house?"

"Oh no, Peter hasn't been up here in years. It was his *father's* studio."

"Oh. Was he an animator, too? Peter doesn't ever talk about his parents. He doesn't ever talk about personal stuff in general. I have to figure it out somehow."

"Their father was a children's book author. He actually won a Caldecott."

"Impressive! Well, this place is spectacular. I would kill for all this space. It'll make a *perfect* art studio."

"Yes, there's even a kitchen and bedroom area in the back. We just need to get it cleaned out and staged."

Ramona watched as Sam walked up to the drawing table. She carefully flipped through a children's book in progress.

"Everything is just as it was."

Sam's eyes widened. "Oh my God! This cat looks just like my cat Vincent!" She held up the drawing. "Kind of weird. Spooky."

She gently set the book down and touched the cat picture, fondly remembering when she adopted Vincent, torn ear and all, in an online auction for an animal rescue organization.

"OK, Ramona. I think I have the perfect twist for Phil's new story."

⤏

Kyle sat at the edge of his bed finger-picking his unplugged Ibanez. He was struggling with a Buddy Guy classic, "What Kind of Woman Is This," and he was trying to get the lick just right.

Suddenly, out of the corner of his eye, he saw the word "NOW" in all caps pop up in a text.

Kyle grabbed his phone. Yup... his dad. He was sure his dad would get the old proverb changed to *Timeliness is next to godliness.*

Kyle stuffed his phone in his pocket and shuffled towards the window. He looked down and saw his best friend Jonesy walking up the driveway, a backpack slung over his shoulder.

Jonesy, earbuds in, nerdier than Kyle but with one foot planted in coolness, shuffled alongside Peter's Tesla, oblivious. Out of his open car window, Peter shouted, "JONESY!"

Jonesy startled. "Shit! Oh hey, Mr. A."

"What are you doing here?"

Jonesy removed his earbuds and fumbled with his backpack. "I just stopped by to... give Kyle a book."

"A book, huh?"

Peter's eyes narrowed. He looked Jonesy up and down, a deer caught in headlights.

Kyle popped open the front door, breaking Jonesy free.

"Hey Jonesy!"

Jonesy looked relieved. "See ya, Mr. A." He darted toward the open door.

"And Kyle... hurry up!" Peter shouted.

Jonesy, face-to-face with Kyle, held up his backpack. "It's in here—"

Kyle yanked him in the door. "Not here. Upstairs."

The two of them ran upstairs. "We've got to be quick," Kyle said.

"Dude, why's your dad so weird?"

"He thinks he's normal."

Kyle walked over to his bedroom window, lowered the blind and twisted the rod. A poster of legendary blues guitarist, Moon, magically appeared. He was in his classic pose, head slung low, fedora tilted, his ebony guitar slung low. The name of his platinum album, "DARK MOON RISIN'" was printed behind him in blazing letters that looked like flames.

Kyle had pasted the poster on the blind, razor-cut along the slats. It appeared and disappeared with a twist of the rod.

Jonesy walked over and stood beside the poster. "Dude, that is dedication." From his backpack, he removed a hat, held it up against the poster.

"BOOM! Dude, it's an exact replica of the hat. This is cool as shit!"

'Where'd you get it?!" Kyle grabbed the hat from Jonesy and planted it on his own head. He grabbed his guitar from under the bed.

"My sister. She works at that vintage clothing shop downtown. That hat is bad-ass on you, man."

"You're my hero. You're kind of a... god."

Jonesy shrugged. "I know."

Kyle's phone buzzed. His dad's text read "NOW!!!"

Kyle clapped Jonesy on the back. He quickly turned back to the window, adjusted the blind to conceal his hero, and said, "We gotta *move*."

They raced down the stairs and flew through the front door and outside. Jonesy headed off to his house, while Kyle, wearing a white button-up shirt with a loosened blue tie, slid into the passenger seat of the Tesla and slammed the door.

He stared blankly out his window. Red headphones collared around his neck, wires hanging like shoestring licorice.

His dad backed out of the driveway, clenching and unclenching his jaw. "Sorry to keep you waiting like that."

Kyle didn't respond to his sarcasm. His dad had this thing about *punctuality* and *planning*. His mother used to joke that the "Two P's" was another thing that pushed them apart. His dad, on the other hand, always complained that his mother considered time as something "fluid." Ten minutes late was nothing to sweat over to his mom. Ten minutes to his dad was a capital offense. Kyle continued staring out the window.

"What did Jonesy want?"

"Nothin'."

"Nothin'? Okaay... soo... Did you finish that report?"

"What?"

"The report. Did you finish it?"

*Oh, yeah. Micromanagement was another classic "Dad" thing.*

"It'll get done. How's Uncle Phil?"

"He's the same. He'll need to take some time off from work to recover. But he'll be fine. Doctor says there are some encouraging signs."

His dad pulled into heavy traffic. Kyle glanced over and saw the little vein in his temple throb. *Here it comes.*

"And *this* is why I tell you to be ready on time. Ten minutes is the difference between sitting in this traffic and getting to your damn school on time. Not to mention having a little courtesy as I still have to get to a meeting after dropping you off."

"Yup." Kyle's voice was monotone.

"And don't try to brush me off. You think getting into med school's some kinda cakewalk? You have got to get into a top-tier college. And doing slacker shit with Jonesy and not finishing projects won't get you there."

"Jonesy is my best friend." Kyle stared out the window.

"We've been over this Kyle. You become the average of the five people you spend time with. Remember?"

Kyle shook his head, facing forward. *Classic Coleridge… Creating a formula for friendship.*

His dad floored the accelerator and darted through traffic. They didn't speak the rest of the way to Kyle's prep school. His dad pulled into the car pool loop.

Kyle grabbed his backpack from the floor in front of him and started to exit.

His dad touched his arm. "So that's it? No, 'Don't worry Dad, I'll take care of it?' Nothing?"

Kyle muttered, "Don't worry, Dad."

Peter shot him a look. "Seriously?! Do you realize how much money this school is costing me? The whole purpose of spending this kind of money on a prep school is—newsflash—to *prep* you for college."

Kyle turned. He could feel his father drilling his eyes into him. Students streamed by. Including Cassidy, from bio. *God, she is perfect. And she sings. Like Janis Joplin. No pretty songbird—grit!*

Kyle finally shot his gaze back to his dad.

"You know what, Dad? Despite what you may think, life's not one of your dumb movies."

Peter rolled his eyes.

"Like, I don't hear any background music. And the last time I checked, people don't always do exactly what *you* want them to do, OK?"

"Exactly, Kyle! Life's not some predictable little ride—"

Kyle looked away and sighed. *Same argument, different day. His dad wouldn't understand him playing guitar if he hit him over the head with his Ibanez.*

"—which is why you have to plan things out. Be diligent—"

His dad looked at him and offered a barely perceptible shake of the head. "Look, just try to be home by six."

"No problem."

Kyle climbed out, slammed the door, and hustled off.

His Dad sped away in his Tesla.

Kyle strode in, worrying about meeting with his guidance counselor. He put his stuff in his locker, checked into homeroom, then headed off to a meeting with Mr. Williams.

First, Kyle waited in an uncomfortable chair outside the guidance office for his appointment time. Mr. Williams was the least-liked school counselor. He never had anything positive to say to anyone. Rumor had it Mr. Williams started a dot.com in Silicon Valley's heyday. He then promptly had a nervous breakdown, cashed out his stocks, took some time off, and eventually went back to school and became a guidance counselor. Everyone said Mr. Williams had so much of his own money, he didn't need to suck up to wealthy parents.

Finally, at the precise minute of his appointment, Mr. Williams opened his office door and ushered Kyle in.

Kyle sank into a plush leather chair while Mr. Williams sat behind his gleaming desk. He looked at his computer, the bluish light reflected in his glasses.

Kyle, nervous, began making chords in the air with his left hand. He'd read in an interview with a blues guitarist in an old *Decca* magazine, about "muscle memories," so he was always practicing. He was determined to perfect his A-SUS chord.

Mr. Williams frowned as he clicked on his keyboard and then leaned even closer to the screen. He narrowed his eyes, just like his dad did when he was about to nag him.

"Well now, Mr. Anderson... I'm looking at your grades here." He pivoted slightly and then folded his hands on his desk. "I'm assuming it will not be front-page news to you that these are *not* pre-medical school grades."

Kyle stopped making air guitar chords and sat up a little straighter.

Mr. Williams adjusted what looked like a very expensive tie, and pushed his glasses further up his nose. "Have you thought about a different major? Not pre-med?"

*A different major.* Kyle tried not to visibly roll his eyes, then muttered, "You're asking the wrong Mr. Anderson."

"Excuse me? What's that you said?"

"So I'mmm… really not the one doing the *thinking* on this."

Kyle expected Mr. Williams to say something mean. But instead he stood and began to pace behind his desk a couple of times, back and forth.

"Mr. Anderson, what is my reputation at school?"

"Huh?" Kyle furrowed his brow.

"Come on. I know what they say about me."

"You do?"

"Yes."

He turned directly toward Kyle and cleared his throat. "Take it from one who knows, Mr. Anderson. You do not do yourself any favors living your life by someone else's vision for it."

*So this was the speech I heard pretty much once a week since I turned five. Who knows, maybe my dad gave me this speech when I was in my mother's stomach. Maybe he pressed his mouth up to her belly and told me this before I was born.*

*Dad's speech—with some minor variations—was always this: Kyle, a man with a plan is a man who succeeds. And in life, you need to have a plan for each hour, each day, each week, each month, each year—and then your whole life. Because life is a long game. Shoot your sights high. Banker. Lawyer. Doctor.*

*He bought me a microscope when I was eight. Well, what kid doesn't like to look at blood, or an ant, or their spit under a microscope slide? But Dad took that as a sign I was gonna be the next Albert Schweitzer.*

*Only problem? By the time I was nine? I was totally over my microscope and was interested in being the next Tom Morello.*

# Stagecraft

*hat does your room say about you?
I feel like if you didn't know me
and walked into my room, it
would tell you a lot about who I am. Over in the corner
rests my Ibanez. My beautiful Ibanez, shiny and perfect.
Over there, my Fender—black, electric, bad ass. I've got
all my vinyl in milk cartons stacked near my desk.*

*Now, my dad had this idea. Uncle Phil didn't need to
go back to his crappy apartment. If he didn't even
remember his apartment, why not give him a new… in the
words of my dad, "scene."*

*Uncle Phil's scene was about to make a dramatic turn.*

Sam stood deciding where to stack a half-dozen
large, blank canvases. She had hired two workers,

and together they had cleaned the loft to gleaming, polishing floors and cabinets, and making it look like an incredibly hip artist studio.

A tech guy and his assistant walked in as other guys brought in boxes. She directed placement of a computer and multiple webcams. The webcams pointed at a large easel and blank canvas.

Sam danced to a salsa recording on her iPhone speakers. Then she paused and folded her arms, arranging elements from some of the boxes by the side of the easel and blank canvas. Old acrylic house paint cans and used brushes, which she placed in funky mason jars splattered with paint colors. She pulled out a large, paint-stained tarp and placed it on the floor.

Next the gates of the elevator opened and a delivery guy appeared at the open door.

Sam turned. "Furniture?"

He nodded. "Yeah, lady."

Sam directed the furniture movers. Then she opened a box labeled, "Cool Clothes." She walked it over to the bedroom space and began hanging Phil's new, all-black "artist" wardrobe. She hung them on expensive silk hangers. She knew Peter had a thing about cheap metal hangers, and about not caring for clothes properly. He had a tailor from Hong Kong, resettled into L.A., who was just as fussy as he was.

Sam continued curating the artist's studio. As she was getting ready to leave, she spotted the trash bag she had brought when she and Ramona had first checked the place out. She realized this bag was especially important, because this bag represented Phil. The real Phil. Though she was trying to support Peter, part of the scheme just bothered her.

She dragged the trash bag of old clothes towards the bedroom space. Opening it, she pulled out a black T-shirt with "I Am Keats" printed in white.

She held it up.

"What is it about Keats that you love so much, Phil?" she whispered to no one in particular. She'd have to ask Ramona what the whole "Keats" thing was all about.

Sam rolled up to the animation studio in her mud-covered Jeep. Music blared—she was currently in a phase of New Orleans jazz-funk. The Neville Brothers echoed, doors off her Jeep, wearing sexy aviator sunglasses, hair wisped across her face. A striking woman. Waiting on the sidewalk in black suit and tie was Peter. He did a double take. *Whoa! That's... Sam?!* As he approached, he assessed the ride he was about to get into and snapped back to reality. He gently hoisted himself up into the passenger seat, being easy on his suit, while trying to display a little... coolness.

"Hey, Peter!" Sam blasted out of the parking lot, Peter bouncing like popcorn, gripping tightly to the roll bar hand strap. His perfectly styled hair bouncing with him.

"Smooth ride... Sammy."

Sam looked over and flashed a big, amused smile. She drove over a pothole, and Peter's head banged into the roof.

"God-dammit!

Sam turned her head to the left, so as not to let Peter see her laugh—though he could see the smirk at the corners of her lips.

Finally, serious-faced, she turned down the music. "Look Peter, I have to be honest with you." She paused, as if to compose her thoughts. "I'm kinda having some difficulty reconciling this 'plan' in my head."

"Don't worry about it. I know Phil better than he knows himself. It'll work out just fine."

"It's not that. It's… the whole thing just *feels* wrong to me."

Peter shifted in his seat, and paused for a moment. "Sam, let me ask you something. Do you think Phil's life, as he was living it, was a good one? Do you think he was really *living*? That he was happy?"

Sam pondered her answer. "Well… not from *my* perspective, but that's irrelevant, right? I mean what I may consider a good life, is subjective. I'm sure people could judge my life and conclude that I'm not really living, or that I'm not happy. But no one knows how someone else really feels."

Peter conceded the point with a slight nod. "Fair enough. But I don't think my assessment of his life is too far off. I really don't. Actions and behaviors are a reflection of how someone feels. And bouncing from one dead-end job to another, living in a cluttered, depressing rent-by-night room, doesn't square in my head as being… 'happy.'"

Sam slowed down, shifting the Jeep smoothly to a stop. "Listen, I 'get it,' but again, it is HIS life. Sure, it's not something *you* would choose, but that's not for you to judge. It's not for any of us." She glanced at him, trying to access his expression.

"Yeah Sam, it *was* his life—but he doesn't *remember* it. Now, could I sit him down and fill his head with everything that's happened in his life since the beginning? Sure. But why should I?"

Sam watched his face.

"Why should I load him down with all of that emotional baggage? He doesn't remember it. And you can't miss something you don't remember, right?"

He observed Sam's skepticism. "Okay look, our memories build our identity, and our reality. They were events that took place in the *past*. But the past *does not exist*. It's simply a bunch of stories we carry around in our heads."

Sam drew a deep breath and shifted the Jeep into gear. Shaking her head, she pulled into traffic.

Peter looked at her and continued. "In other words Sam, all of our experiences in life are filed away in our minds. We take those events, especially ones charged with emotion, and we allow them to shape who we are, where we go in life."

Peter studied Sam's profile. "So, if Phil has had a lot of heartache, those emotions stay attached to the memories of the events." He extended his index finger in the air to begin his count down.

"This causes a depressed state of mind."

Second finger: "Which then colors his perceptions and affects his behavior."

Third finger: "Which in turn is being viewed, and judged by the world."

Fourth finger: "And this reaction by others further affects his mood and exacerbates his negative feelings about himself."

He rested his hand in his lap. "Do you see how this is a vicious cycle, a self-fulfilling prophecy. It's like a conditioned 'script' that his mind keeps playing, over and over. If we're able to stop that script and introduce Phil to a new one, it will give him a fighting chance."

Sam searched for a rebuttal, but came up empty. She swerved to avoid a pothole full of water. Peter seized on a philosophical opportunity.

"Sam, you just swerved around that puddle so you wouldn't splash it up on those people, right?"

"Yeah? So?"

"So later today, when the sun has dried up the water, is it still a... puddle?"

"What?" She glanced at him, eyebrow raised.

"Well, a few seconds ago, in the *past*, it was a puddle. At least it was to you. To the sparrows it was a birdbath. To the stray dog, it was a bowl of water. This afternoon, after the water has evaporated, what will it be? A pothole?"

"I understand what you're getting at, but it certainly existed. You said the past doesn't exist."

"It doesn't 'exist.' It *happened*. Everything is a happening, Sam. There are no static, separate things. That puddle is defined by its relationships, its interactions. It only 'exists' in the minds of those who've experienced it, and only if it mattered to them."

Sam stared straight ahead. "Okay, you're losing me…"

"Look, most people will have no memory at all of that puddle. But if you had splashed it up on a guy heading to a job interview, I can assure you that *happening* will take on meaning and 'exist.' But… it only exists as a thought in *his* head."

Sam furrowed her brow.

"I know it sounds like zen, like a *koan*. But just think about it, Sam."

⌇

*The road to hell is paved with good intentions.*

*I never truly understood what that meant… until I experienced it. What my dad was unable to understand was that his intentions, regardless of whether they were well meaning, have consequences. And sometimes the intent and consequence doesn't square up.*

*After the death of my grandparents, my dad became the "adult." He assumed responsibility of Uncle Phil and decided that he needed to "guide" him through life. Unfortunately, he didn't comprehend that my uncle had a mind of his own. Uncle Phil needed his big brother, emotionally, but my dad couldn't see that because he was so blinded by this immense responsibility that he decided he needed to take on. So he proceeded to run Uncle Phil's life, as he felt best, all the while he was oblivious to the fact that Uncle Phil was rebelling against everything my dad tried to do, even at his own peril. That old saying, "cut off his nose to spite his face," yep, that was Uncle Phil. But my dad never understood that Uncle Phil's failures were a direct consequence of my dad's need to control his life. Intent versus consequence. So now, my dad saw an opportunity to fix the life that Uncle Phil screwed up by not listening to him in the first place. For such a brilliant guy, my father can do some really dumb shit.*

They finally arrived at the loft. Sam undid her seatbelt and jumped out the side. Peter did the same. Well, kinda. The whole Jeep without doors things was an acquired taste. One he didn't suspect he would be acquiring any time soon.

Peter began to frantically bat at his head in an attempt to tame his hair into something somewhat presentable. He neatened his suit, glanced down and did a double take at what he saw all over his pant legs—of his *good* suit. White cat hair!? He looked at Sam then back down at his pants, then shook his head in disgust. "What the——?!"

"Seriously? You need to relax."

Sam shook her head as they walk into the building. They rode up in silence. Peter fussed with the offending cat hair. She decided to let Peter obsess and pout in peace. She unlocked the door to the loft and Peter slowly followed.

His father's old studio. It felt like entering a church, as if he needed to pay his respects, be reverent. There was a lump in his throat, and he was having difficulty catching his breath. He almost forgot about the cat hair.

Sam grabbed a roll of tape from a desk, ripped off a bunch, got on her knees and started cleaning off Peter's pant leg.

"It's just a little cat hair."

Peter, brought out of his reverie, irritated and uncomfortable, yanked his leg away. "Uh-huh... OK, that's good. And why the hell is there cat hair all over your Jeep anyway?"

"That's Vincent's outdoor bed."

Peter rolled his eyes. He shifted gears back to the nostalgia he was feeling. It was like he had stepped back in time. His father's old space. God... what emotions. Though it looked different, it still smelled the same. Felt the same. He saw he and Phil playing cars on the beautiful, shiny wood floors with the sun streaming in. He could hear his dad's voice, smell the coffee, and he could feel how he felt safe... and loved. He took a few steps, looked around at the loft. He was impressed with what Sam had done. Sam gazed up at him, trying to assess his reaction, his eyes distant, impossible to read.

"What'd ya think?"

Peter attempted to hide just how impressed he was. "Not bad."

He continued to take it all in, though. Every beam, every window pulled him into the past. His father's old space. He glanced at the island near the kitchen and saw him and Phil, each sitting on a barstool, legs dangling, a giant ice cream sundae in front of each of them. Their dad had swirled whipped cream on their sundaes and then squirted a dab of cream on each boy's nose. Peter remembered what a treat visits to the loft entailed. His father loved to show off his drawings, and let him and Phil play with paints and charcoal sketches. They ate ice cream for dinner, and his dad told them it was "Guys' Night."

Sam reached out and took him by the arm. "Follow me. I want to show you some things." Sam pointed out the webcams, the computer. And finally, the easel and canvas. "I left it blank."

Peter was irritated by the plain white canvas. "What?! C'mon, you should've at least got him started."

"Started? I don't know what interests him. You showed me a crayon drawing from when you two were little boys. Can he even paint?"

"I don't know. And it doesn't matter. Remember, *he* doesn't know what interests him."

Peter's eyes followed wires running up the walls. "And what's with the webcams again? Am I missing something?"

"Listen, you said 'just make it happen.' So, I'm making it happen."

She beckoned with her index finger. "Here, take a look."

Sam led Peter over to a computer and punched up a website. Suddenly Peter was looking at a live stream of the loft. Peter turned around and waved his hand at a webcam. *Hey… that's me!*

"Are we streaming live?!"

"Yeah, so here's how it works." She leaned over the keyboard and pressed some keys and pointed at the screen.

Peter leaned in to the computer monitor, the glow lighting up his glasses. He tried to understand Sam's vision for the loft, for the whole plan. He sat at the computer, scrolling through Phil's new website. Sam stood next to him, coaching and walking him through the site map.

"Look Sam, I really don't understand what you're doing." He reached into his inside breast pocket and pulled out his Italian leather wallet. "But here——" He pulled out one of his platinum credit cards.

"Buy a couple of paintings, so he thinks he's *actually* a professional artist."

The card hung in the air between them.

Sam crossed her arms. "You don't get it, do you? You gave me a ridiculous project. Help rewrite your brother's story. Make him a happy-go-lucky artist."

"Yeah?"

"So, Story Man? Where are all of these paintings he's supposedly created over the years? What if he wants to see them? Are they in a gallery somewhere?"

"I never really thought about that——"

"Well, I have. That's why we're selling through an online auction. Because after your eccentric, artist brother finishes a painting, he never wants to see it again. He thinks it 'interferes with his spontaneous creativity.' Right out of his man, Keats. So... he secures the money transfer, packs it up, ships it off."

She affected a wave. "Bye-bye. Gone. Forever. Make sense?"

Peter nodded. "Makes sense, but how's anyone going to find his website? And better yet, why would they ever buy whatever it is he creates?"

"One ruse at a time, OK? I'm working on it."

She exhaled and stared straight into Peter's eyes.

"What?" he asked. "Why are you looking at me like that?"

"Peter, have you even considered that Phil won't play along? What if he doesn't *want* to paint? Your whole scheme will go out the window. All this work."

"Don't worry. I have absolutely *no* doubt that Phil will go along."

Sam gave him a skeptical look.

"Look, Sam… who we think we are is a mental construct. We *become* the stories we tell ourselves."

"Oh right, *now* I'm clear."

"Think about what we do for a living. We make shit up. More than that, we make people *believe* those stories. Remember when we did *Oscar's Dream?*"

"You mean the… kitchen appliances as dysfunctional family movie?"

"Right. Well, we got so many fan emails and letters from people who *swore* the family and Oscar and all of it was *them*. Cartoon kitchen appliances, for cripes' sake! They related to every bit of it. We *live* the stories we tell, Sam. We're just not aware of it. And that's why I had that moment in the conference room. I could see it all so clearly. The problem was Phil's attachment to his personal fiction. He was being who he thought others thought he was. The guy who doesn't care about anything. The guy who is a failure. Who doesn't *care* that he's a failure. A slacker. That was his old story. His brain was using his past, his memories, to strengthen that story and create his present. But now, they're gone. And so we can create a *new* present for him—a new *story* with new experiences—which will become the seeds for his life moving forward."

Sam squinted at him. "I don't think the things I know about myself are made up."

"You don't, huh. OK, when you were a kid did your parents ever tell you that you were... I dunno... talented?"

"Sure. I was dancing at age five."

"And how did that make you feel?"

"It made me feel good. So what?"

"So you probably wanted more of that feeling, and... "

"Let me guess—"

Peter held up a hand. "You don't have to guess. You know. To get more of those feelings, you..." He could see her face was registering mild shock. "Look, we all do it. We do the dance, no pun intended. We end up becoming an accumulation of everyone else's ideas of who they think we are, of who we should be."

Peter stood up, walked over, and straightened the blank canvas on the easel, just so. "So do I think that once he starts selling paintings and people start noticing him, especially you and me, that he'll want more and more of that... story?"

As Peter spoke, Sam walked over to Peter's father's drafting table and carefully gathered up the unfinished children's book.

"Peter?"

Peter turned. She looked at him with an earnest gaze, and held out the drawings.

"Please take these home. I don't want anything to happen to them."

Peter froze. He recognized his father's pen and ink style. He swallowed. He felt a stabbing pain in his chest just looking at them. Finally, he walked over to Sam.

"And here——" She put the drawings down and grabbed a suit bag from a hook on the wall. "New clothes for when Phil leaves the hospital. Best I could do with what I had to work with."

The next morning, Peter woke. His brother's new clothes hung in a bag on his closet door. Phil still had no memories. And now they were jumping in with both feet.

Peter dressed, feeling oddly nervous. He chalked it up to both bringing his brother home from the hospital, and anticipation. He was about to rewrite his brother's story, and if all went well, his brother could at last lead a life worth living—full of creativity and meaning and more, instead of toiling for some barely-above-minimum-wage job that did not appreciate Phil's innate gifts.

After picking up Sam, driving to the hospital, and meeting with Doctor Singh, Peter anxiously waited as a nurse helped Phil dress, and wheeled him to the lobby in a wheelchair, dressed stylishly in all black. Peter offered a wave. "I'll take it from here," he said.

Peter steered his brother to the curb. Sam stood next to Peter's car, walked over to Phil, and extended her hand.

"Hi Phil. I'm... Sam."

"Hey. My brother didn't tell me he was married."

"We're not." She flushed. "We work together. Um. I work for him."

"My mistake. You two just looked like you belong together, that's all. Sam was it?"

Sam looked up at Peter. He rolled his eyes. *Belong together. Whatever.*

They all got settled into the Tesla, and left the hospital.

"I bet it feels good to be going home," Sam offered.

"Well, being as I don't know where home is, I don't know. But it will be nice to have some privacy, and no nursing staff and doctors poking at me every few hours and strapping me into machines."

Peter drove through downtown to the loft. He parked on the street, and unlocked the car doors.

"This way into the building," Sam said. They entered the building and then the industrial elevator.

"What floor am I on?" Phil asked.

"Third." Sam said. "It gets the most ambient light."

She unlocked the door to the loft and swung the heavy door wide. She handed Phil the key ring with an artist's palette charm on it. "And these are your keys."

Over Phil's head, Peter mouthed *nice touch.*

They walked in and Peter, just as he had the day before, felt a surge of recognition and emotion seeing his father's studio. He cleared his throat. "Is it coming back to you, bro?"

"Not really, no." Phil looked around, an expression of seeming awe on his face.

Sam walked in. "Most of the space is obvious. Your kitchen is over there. You have the sleeping space over there," she gestured. "I stocked your fridge with all the things you like. Wheat grass, carrot juice. Lots of fruit. Raw veggies. Your juicer is over there on the counter."

"I like vegetables? And carrot juice?"

"Yes. You live very healthy."

Phil patted his stomach. "Then why do I have this spare tire, here?"

Peter's eyes widened. He looked at Sam with a "fix this" expression.

Sam laughed. "You have a weakness for ice cream. But you were on a health kick again, really strict. In fact, it's why you were on that bike trip. You'll be back in fighting form in no time."

"What's with the cameras?"

"Those? Yeah, you're against having any public presence, other than your website. People bid while you're painting. Then you sell it, and it's... gone." She waved her hand as if depicting a puff of smoke. "You said it's like Buddhists sweeping away their sand mandalas."

Phil walked over to the large, blank canvas and stared.

"Really? What do I... paint?"

Sam exhaled. "Hmm. It's hard to describe."

Sam glanced over at Peter, who shrugged. She was the point person on this.

"Try," Phil said.

"Okaaay... so... I'd say a combination of abstract expressionism, surrealism. Maybe a touch of... neo-expressionism. Early Philip Guston? Maybe some... Rothko? Basquiat? It's really difficult to pigeonhole you, Phil."

"Huh."

"Yes! You know why? Your work evolves, it's... dynamic. *You're* dynamic!"

Sam caught Peter's gaze and lifted her eyebrows.

Peter responded, impressed by both the backstory she created for his brother, as well as her improv skills. "You're shaking up the art world."

"Oh, OK... anyway, I'm starving. I've had enough apple sauce and fluorescent Jell-O for a lifetime. Can we go grab a bite?"

Peter put his hand on Phil's shoulder. "We'll go out for your favorite!"

Phil stared at him blankly.

Peter paused, smiled. "Wait... that's right! You can't remember. Don't worry, bro... you love it."

The three of them left the loft and headed to a deli down the block. Sam reminded Phil, "You usually get the cobb salad. You know. Healthy."

When they entered, the hostess did a double-take. Staring at Peter, she grabbed three menus. As she led them to a booth, a hushed whisper settled over the lunchtime crowd.

"Isn't that Peter Anderson? That's Peter Anderson. That's him..."

Peter tried to ignore it. They sat down and took the offered menus, Sam and Peter sitting across from Phil. Peter glanced at his watch. He had spent way more time than he really could afford dealing with all this Phil stuff—particularly since the movie seemed to be getting bogged down. And if he never had to deal with Zack again, it would be too soon.

Phil slowly lifted his head, peering over his menu. A booth full of guys in lime green shirts stared back at him. He lowered his head, then peered back over the menu. Finally, he looked at Peter, covering his mouth with his menu.

"Psst. Pete! Why are those guys looking over here? Do they know me?"

Peter snapped his head around, seeing the ridiculous House Warehouse attire. *Aww shit!* He turned back to Phil.

"I have no idea. You definitely have a following."

Peter elbowed Sam. "Do me a favor. Go see what those guys want."

"Excuse me?!"

"Maybe they know you from the House Warehouse? You shop there, right? The place with the green walls," Peter nudged.

"I really think they were looking at me," Phil whispered from behind the menu. "No offense, Sam. You're very beautiful and all, but they seem to be staring at me."

"No offense, bro, but I don't think you're their type."

Peter nodded toward the table. "Go ahead, Sam. Make their day."

A baffled-looking Sam slowly pushed herself from the table. She turned and saw one of the Warehouse guys walking toward them. She quickly stepped in front of him. He peered around her, ignoring her attempt to engage him. His gaze was fixated on Phil.

"Phil! Is that you? We wondered what happened after Chester canned you——"

Sam leaned her face close to his and then glanced at his nametag. "Hey, how are you... Jerry?"

The guy's voice suddenly had a flirtatious edge. "Hey yourself. I see you're with Phil over there? You guys friends or somethin'?"

"Who?" Sam looked back at the table, smiled, and waved at Phil. "Oh, Phil? Yes. Actually, Phil and I are a lot *more* than friends, if you... *know* what I mean."

Sam turned the stunned Warehouse guy around and led him back to his coworkers.

Phil, meanwhile, had watched the entire exchange with interest. "Bro, who was that? He seemed to know me. Maybe if I go talk to him, it'll jog my memory or——"

"Look Phil, let's take things slow. You just got out of the hospital. I'm sure Sam'll grab his card. And we can call him once you've had some time to recoup.

Maybe after a few memories start coming back. OK? Like you don't even know if that is some stalker, or obsessed art fan. You don't know if that guy once tried to rip you off. So maybe once a few things start coming back to you... you know?"

Sam sashayed back to the table and sat down.

"So, how does that guy know me?"

"Actually Phil, he realized you weren't who he thought you were."

Peter lifted up his menu. First crisis averted. And they hadn't even made it through lunch.

*I've given a lot of thought to my dad's idea about stories people tell themselves. And I am pretty sure what I think would make his head explode.*

*See, here's the thing. My dad was hellbent on me getting into medical school. So my story? The story I was told over and over when I was a kid, was: "You like to help people. You're going to be a doctor."*

*But I kind of had a problem with that story. Deep, deep down, in the part of yourself where you just know if something is a lie or not, I knew that story was not true. I was not meant to be a doctor.*

*Instead, my truest me was the guy who played the guitar, lost in riffs, lost in the strings. Arpeggiating scales and making them dance.*

*But at that moment in time, I could never have told my dad that. Because he was still being Peter Anderson. He was the scriptwriter. And we were all actors in his movie. He was writing the stories for us.*

*He was writing one for Uncle Phil.*

*And he was writing one for me.*

*But the problem—the big problem, the proverbial elephant in the room? Did he have a right to do that?*

*All I knew was I wanted to write my own story.*

*My own song.*

# The Price is Right

*T*he moon rises.

*No one tells the moon to rise.*

*But there it is. A sliver of a silver dangling impossibly in a starry sky. Or a half-moon, hiding some of its beauty in the shadows. Or Pink Floyd's Dark Side of the Moon. And then, sometimes you look up and the moon is a sphere, this brilliant rock in the sky, daring you to look at it.*

*But it rises on its own. And no one has to tell the moon to do its dance with the tides.*

*But Dad thinks he can control everything. Maybe even the moon.*

*And I have one word—well, two—for Dad.*

*Leap year.*

*Because even the atomic clock and all that—all that man-made stuff of time and place? It isn't perfect. And every once in a while, February gets an extra day.*

*Doesn't that show, you can't control it all? Even the Universe won't totally conform to what man is dictating.*

*But Dad is one of those guys who says, "Don't tell me about the stumbling blocks. Show me the finished product. Yesterday."*

*And he was getting really anxious that this idea he'd dreamed and schemed wasn't going according to plan.*

*And the great Peter Anderson thrived on plans. And most especially thrived on them going precisely how he wanted them to.*

Peter, lacking sleep, needed a second coffee. He never needed a second coffee. He buzzed Sam to bring him one, but then decided to cut to the chase and go to the cappuccino machine himself.

He exited his office, and there was Sam, sitting at her desk looking at Phil's website. Peter looked over her shoulder at the screen.

"What's Wonder Artist doing now?"

"The same thing he's been doing for the past two days." She glanced up at Peter and laughed. "Looks like your creature has a mind of his own, Dr. Frankenstein."

Peter and Sam leaned in. Peter was incredulous. Was he really seeing what he was seeing?

Phil danced shirtless around the loft, wearing a flowing silk cape, waving a paint-covered brush like a symphony director. Paint flew everywhere, like a Jackson Pollock come to life.

"What's he wearing... a fucking cape?! A cape?"

He leaned in closer, not trusting his eyes.

"And what's up with his hair? Is it... white?! Peroxided?"

"Spiked up pretty good too."

"He's just confused. I'll set him straight when I see him."

"Oh, he's confused all right."

"So, have you created any fake buyers yet?"

"Just getting ready to place a bid on... Master Phil Anderson. Anyway, we're all set to go. How much do you want me to spend on his first painting?"

"I don't care. A few hundred? It doesn't really matter. I put enough money in his account to last a while... So just take care of it."

Peter turned, walked back to his office, shaking his head. "I just hope the idiot eventually *paints* something."

Sam found herself addicted to watching Phil online. It was better than any reality show—not that she watched that crap. Still, she sat there amused, clicking on Phil's website, placing fake bids.

About twenty minutes later, Dan Adams strolled through the front entrance of the studio. She could see him through the glass doors, checking in with the security desk.

Tall, charismatic, movie-star handsome, he sauntered toward her like he owned the place—which he kinda did. A former celebrity athlete, entrepreneur, and major investor in Peter's company, Dan always got everything he wanted... well, except for Sam.

Dan sneaked up on Sam at her computer and tickled her side.

"Sam, you gorgeous creature. Big Dan's here to make your day."

"Ah, Dan. How are *you*?"

Dan leaned over the desk. "Oops? Whatcha doing baby, shopping?" He leaned closer to her ear and said softly. "Look, you do whatever you want. Tell Peter I said so."

"No, no I'm just… taking a break, looking at a friend's new painting on his website."

"Really? Let me see… You know, I'm somewhat of a collector."

Dan hovered over Sam's shoulder. Phil was lying on the floor. Wearing only plaid briefs and a cape, paint all over his body.

"Is that… the artist?"

She had to keep herself from laughing. "Yes. I know. Unorthodox. But he's quite brilliant, a bit… eccentric."

"Yeah, this is strange. Where's the painting?"

Sam pointed. "It's right there. See? In the corner."

Sam clicked on an icon and switched webcams. The image on the monitor now zoomed into the dreadful mess on canvas. A color-clashing, overly aggressive finger painting.

"It's pretty cool, really. The buyer never knows what they're buying until the painting's finished and the bidding ends. It's all about, for him, creating art in the moment."

"*Verry* interesting. What's the bidding up to on *that* one?"

Sam pointed to the bidding. "Oh, it's only just begun. It's at, uhh, five hundred."

"Well, I'll tell you what, Sam. Big Dan is going to buy this one for my collection, as a favor to you and your friend. Once my friends see it, guarantee you, his cachet in the art world will go way up."

Sam's eyes widened. "Are you serious?" She looked back at the painting. It was awful.

"To show you how serious I am, I'll place a bid at... say... 10 thousand. That should get it, don't ya think?"

Sam felt panic bubbling to the surface. "Oh, no Dan. Please. You don't have to do that."

Dan removed his credit card from his wallet and handed it to Sam.

"I know I don't *have* to do it. Big Dan doesn't *have* to do anything. I *want* to do it. For you."

Sam wondered if her entire face had gone pale. Could he hear her heart pounding?

"Anyway," Dan continued. "I'm a bit of a savant at discovering up-and-coming artists. Bet you didn't know that."

"No, I didn't. You're something else."

Sam jotted down his credit card info and returned his card.

"Thank you, Dan. I owe you one."

Peter exited his office.

"Dan! Good to see you, my friend. I've got those numbers you were looking for."

Dan winked at Sam. "Talk to you later, baby. Big Dan's got some problems to solve."

As Dan and Peter walked away, Sam turned back to her desk and rolled her eyes.

Suddenly, Dan stopped. "Oh and Sam, I almost forgot. I'm having a party next Friday. How 'bout returning the favor and stopping by?"

"Oh, I don't know—"

Peter nodded. "You should go. You don't get out enough, especially with all the work you've been putting in on that *special* project. Go. Have a little fun."

Sam shot Peter a dirty look.

She looked at Dan. "OK, but can I bring a friend?"

"Sure thing. The more, the merrier."

"Great." She forced enthusiasm into her voice. "See you then!"

Sam returned to watching Phil and trying not to be so distracted that she didn't do her other work. While she was at lunch, she missed Dan leaving. When she got back, she poked her head in Peter's office.

"Back. Need anything?"

"Um. Sit down for a minute."

She sat opposite his desk and crossed her arms.

"So…" Peter grinned broadly. "What favor are you returning for Dan?"

"Oh, you know, I'm not sure you'll believe it."

"Try me."

"Let's see… only the fact that he purchased Phil's first painting."

"No kidding? Phil painted something? How 'bout that."

"If that's what you'd call what ended up on the canvas."

"How much did Dan bid?"

"Guess?" She grinned like the Cheshire Cat."

"You know I never play guessing games. Come on. Five hundred?"

"More."

"You're kidding. All right, how should I know? Just tell me."

"Let's see, I think it was... ten grand?"

Peter's face registered abject shock.

"What!?"

"Yup."

"Aww shit, don't let Dan waste his money like that. Just to impress you. This may spin back around on us."

Sam raised her eyebrows. "You're *just* thinking about this now? Now?!"

"Well..." Peter stammered.

"And about your semantics... On us? Us?!"

"OK. Us. Me. Whatever..." He looked down at some papers on his desk. "You know—" Peter fidgeted with his pens and pencils, lining them up carefully, all parallel, in a row. "—there isn't a woman around who wouldn't jump at the opportunity to be with Dan. He's generous to a fault—he just proved that to you. I really can't understand why you two don't get together. He's a decent guy."

"You really don't get me, do you? Like... I've sat outside your office for years, and you *still* don't get me."

"You've never thought about the kind of life this guy could give you? He lunches at The Ivy. He gets an invite to the Vanity Fair Oscars party every year. He travels the world. And he really—OK, he's occasionally a little arrogant—but he has a great sense of humor. And did I mention… he's loaded?"

"You mean, I should get involved with him because he'd… what?… indulge my obsession with Prada handbags? Are you being serious right now?"

Peter suddenly looked flustered and opened his desk drawer as if looking for another pen. "I didn't mean it that way. It's just that… Look, forget I said anything. I just overheard the 'return the favor' thing and—"

"Please shut up and quit while you are behind. I get it, you're confused. Probably because of the types of women you get involved with. Just sayin'… they love that black Amex."

Peter opened his mouth to say something, then appeared to change his mind.

"Anyway, you're coming with me."

"To Big Dan's? Sorry, no can do. But… this could be a great opportunity for you to introduce Phil to his new 'artist' life. What do you think?"

Sam stared at Peter. Peter raised his eyebrows and smiled. "Gotta admit, hanging out with that kind of crowd of important people? It'll be good for him."

Sam raised her eyebrows, but shook her head. After years of experience, she knew better than to argue with a Peter brainstorm. When he got an idea, he was tenacious. She couldn't recall a single time in all the years she'd been by his side, when he changed his mind or changed course. Once a plan was made, he would drive that train right through a wall if need be.

"OK, Phil," she muttered under her breath. "Looks like it's gonna be you and me."

Sam drove her Jeep, enjoying the California sun on her face. No humidity, not a cloud in the sky.

Her phone rang. On the display: "Boss." She answered. "Hey Peter, what's up?"

"What's up? I'm watching my idiot brother on his website, that's what's up. Just checking to make sure you don't need anything, and that everything's goin' as planned."

"As planned or as imagined?"

"Smart ass."

"I'm on my way over there right now."

"Holy shit!"

"What?" Sam furrowed her brow.

"Now he's naked from the waist up and he's *throwing* paint. Throwing it! Like he's a warm-up pitcher for the Giants."

"All right, take it easy. I'll be there soon and you'll be able to watch as I try to wrangle your brother into acting… I don't know. Normal? I told you he wouldn't follow your script."

"Just check in with me later. Let me know how he's doin'."

The call disconnected, but Sam addressed her phone. "Peter, this crazy train has left the station."

When she arrived at the loft, she parked her Jeep and headed into the building. The door to the studio was cracked open. Sam walked in, finding Phil—just as Peter described him—naked from the waist up, dancing to—was that House of Pain?—and throwing paint-soaked rags at the painting Big Dan bought.

"Hey, Phil."

He turned around with a huge grin on his face.

"Um, what's going on? With the throwing paint stuff?

Phil was covered in splotches of paint—on his stomach, face, chest, arms. His hands were completely blue and purple.

"Sam! You're not going to believe this! Someone bid ten thousand dollars for my painting. I'm just finishing it up. And then I guess I'll... *pack* it up!"

"That's wonderful! But you don't have to pack it. One of Peter's investors noticed your work and bought it. In fact, we've been invited to his house for a party Friday night. So we'll just bring it with us and you can hand it to him. OK? Lots easier this time."

"OK, great! But..." He turned to face the canvas. "I was wondering. Is ten thousand a lot? I mean... what were my paintings selling for *before*?"

"Funny that you ask. You've always been an artist who is all about the *creative* forces. You never mentioned your prices... to anyone. You couldn't have cared less. The highest bidder got the painting. End of story."

She gestured around the loft. "But this is prime real estate. So clearly you were doing pretty darn well."

"No shit?! Well, maybe ten grand is a *deal* then. I did feel inspired with this one."

He put down the rag he held and then walked to the kitchen sink to wash. "So Sam... you think you could help me pick out something to wear to the party?"

"Sure. Let's take a look."

He finished scrubbing his hands, which were still a pale bluish color. He dried them on a dish towel, and then led the way to the bedroom area, which was blocked off with a rolling rice paper screen.

Sam opened the built-in closet, sliding an assortment of all-black clothing along the rod. Phil stood, arms folded over his paint-covered chest, curious.

Sam paused on various pieces, shaking her head, moving on. Big Dan partied with a total A-list crowd.

Finally, she arrived at the now-laundered and pressed "I am Keats" T-shirt. A tiny smile appeared on her face as she lifted it off the rod.

"That's mine?" Phil's eyes widened.

"Yes. Of course. You love... um, Keats's ability to embrace uncertainty. He embodies your approach to painting."

"Cool."

She put the Keats T-shirt back and pulled out a black turtleneck. "How about this for the party? With black pants. Very basic, classy."

"All right, then. What time Friday night?"

"I'll pick up you—and the painting—around 8:00. OK?"

He nodded and reached out, grabbing the Keats T-shirt from the closet. Sam wondered if that was a flicker of recognition in his eyes.

Friday arrived. Sam dressed in a black mini-skirt, gold sandals, a diaphanous top, and her hair tumbled in loose waves.

She picked Phil up, expecting he might have chosen to wear the Keats shirt. Instead, he emerged in front of his building in an artist's outfit straight out of central casting. He wore the black pants and black turtleneck she suggested. But he had added a black leather jacket, and funky, yellow-rimmed glasses.

"Well," Sam muttered under her breath. "That's certainly an interesting choice."

She waved at Phil, who climbed in the front seat of her Jeep, placing his four-foot square painting in the back. When he turned his head to put the painting there, Sam gasped.

"What?" Phil looked back at the painting. Then turned and faced Sam, confused.

"Um. Nothing."

"Oh. This?" He patted the side of his head. He had shaved lightning bolts into his hair, which already dyed platinum. "I felt like it was me, Sam. I feel like I am learning more about who I am. This is me. Wouldn't you say so?"

Sam, still stunned, just nodded. She swallowed, and then said, "Let's go, shall we? I'm sure you'll be a hit at the party. Big Dan loves your work."

Bob Dylan's "Lay Lady Lay" poured from the speakers. Phil, relaxed, tried to sing along.

"Lay lady lay. Lay across my big breast, babe."

Sam glanced over and smiled, wondering if it was worth it to even tell him he had the words wrong. She decided to let it go.

"So how you doin', Phil?"

"I'm doin' good."

"Love the outfit, by the way."

"Why thank you. You're looking quite lovely yourself."

She smiled, enjoying the fresh air.

"Sam?"

"Yeah?"

"Do me a favor, would ya?"

"Sure."

"Please don't call me Phil anymore."

"What?"

"Yeah." He straightened in the passenger seat. "It doesn't feel right to me."

"Okaay."

Next to her, he began mouthing his name.

"Phill. Philllll. Feeel. Phil." He stretched his mouth, reminding her of an opera singer warming up before staging *Madame Butterfly*. He spread his mouth wide, then tapped at his Adam's apple.

He offered her a sidelong glance. "Yeah... it's not right. From now on, call me... Keats. I'm the artist known as Keats!"

Sam wondered. Was he recovering his memories, the guy who he used to be?

"Keats?"

"Yeah, just Keats."

"OK... Keats."

"Thanks, Sam."

She turned off an exit. "If you don't mind me asking, why Keats?"

"I really don't know. I saw that T-shirt in my closet. The one you pulled out. And, I just... I felt like it was a moment of recognition, Sam. Like, for a brief moment, maybe Keats was part of my old life. I like Keats as my new name. I dunno. Why not, right?"

"Why not?"

"And could you do me another favor?"

"Sure."

"Change my website to let people know that... I am Keats? You're good at that computer stuff, right?"

"No problem, Phil... um, Keats. I'll make a quick update as soon as we get to Dan's."

Sam shifted into second gear and climbed up into the hills. Her Jeep ran through a neighborhood of luxurious homes, offering sweeping views of the ocean, glimmering lights of downtown.

Suddenly, a gust of wind picked up Phil's painting and carried it off like a magic carpet. Sam and Phil were oblivious.

Eventually, Sam pulled up to Big Dan's house. It was damn impressive from its French Country stonework, to its expansive lawns, its incredible flowering jasmine, infinity pool glimpsed from the drive, and its view.

Sam let out a low whistle. "Not bad."

"Sure. Not bad. But I gotta tell ya… I'm having a sort of déjà vu or somethin'. Did I ever live up here?"

Sam swallowed. "I don't think so. Since I've known you, you've lived at your loft."

"Hmm. Strange."

Sam put the Jeep into park. "Yeah. So let's go in."

"Wait. You have to admit, this is pretty weird. Like, I don't remember who I am. Let alone remember Peter. This is so confusing. So tell me. How well do you know my brother?"

"Pretty well, I guess. I've been working with him for almost five years. He's an awesome boss, but pretty… exacting. Everything has to be spelled out, planned out, charted out, put into an Excel spreadsheet, then put into a report." She laughed.

"I feel like I know this. Has he always been a little… I dunno… anal and uptight?"

Sam smiled. "Kinda. I guess I am used to it. But to be fair to Peter, he *has* been under a *lot* of pressure. First of all, there was your horrible accident, and wanting to be sure you are OK. Then there's Kyle. And then work."

"Work? I thought he was some big shot. Mr. Perfect. Mr. Entrepreneur."

"Sure. But I mean, the new film is *way* behind schedule. It's quite possible his investors will pull the plug. And that will be the literal kiss of death to this movie, and maybe his studio."

"God! I'm sorry to hear all that." He looked out at the view. "I feel kind of guilty for contributing to this."

"Listen. You had nothing to do with it. You had a bad accident. I won't lie. Has this stressed Peter out? Of course. But that's just because he cares about you."

"If the studio went bankrupt, what would happen to you?"

"Honestly? I finally decided to buy a condo. Housing prices weren't getting any lower. If we went belly up, I'd have to land a new job pretty quickly."

"And this McMansion. You said this guy *Dan* is an investor?"

"Yeah, he's one of the biggest... unfortunately."

"I take it you're not a fan?"

"Not really my kinda guy."

"How come?"

"He has a little too much opinion and swagger for my taste. Dan Adams wants whatever's best for Dan Adams. And he'll do whatever he has to do to get it. Definitely not my type."

Sam pulled the keys out of the ignition. Other people, in California "chic" clothes, walked by them toward the house.

"So... what about you and Pete?"

"P-peter?" she sputtered.

"What's going on there? I've seen how he looks at you. At first I thought you were his wife. Then his girlfriend. I mean, even a guy with amnesia can see it," he joked.

"Are you *kidding* me? You really *don't* remember a thing, do you? Peter's great but... Let's change the subject. OK?"

"OK. And I *do* hope it all works out, with the movie and all. I mean, what will the world do without a talking toaster oven?"

"He's a toaster, Phil."

"Tomato, tamato."

"Yeah, I suppose. First-world problems, right? Talking toaster, abstract art..."

Sam looked in the rearview mirror for Phil's painting. Her eyes widened. *Shit! Where'd it go!* "Phil... we have a teensy problem. Well, a ten-thousand-dollar problem."

Phil whipped his head around. "Uh-oh."

She put the keys back in the ignition and put the Jeep in reverse. "We have to retrace our route. Your painting must have bounced out."

She backtracked her precise route to Dan's, while Phil looked for the painting. They found the canvas by the side of the road, smack in the middle of some bushes. Sam chuckled to herself. Someone could have plucked it from the bushes and kept it. But who would want that thing?

Phil hopped out and grabbed the painting. He placed it in the back seat.

"Did anything happen to it?"

"No. It's fine. Almost as if the fates wanted us to find it again."

Sam smiled, and they headed back to Dan's McMansion. Sam had been to France—studied abroad one semester, and then returned for a vacation one year. Dan could call his mansion French Country all he wanted. He could even have all that ivy, tended by gardeners, climbing the faux tower. But it would never be classic and would always be a very poor imitation of what the beauty of French architecture actually embodied.

Sam and Phil walked up the front path, passing three Porsches, two BMWs, and a garish yellow Lamborghini. Phil held his painting over his head.

They stopped at the front door. Sam looked for the doorbell, but before she could press it, the door swung open. A server dressed in all black showed them in, pointing out the extensive buffet table, complete with a raw bar and a scantily clad young woman in a bikini, shucking oysters. There were two bars. One inside, one out by the pool.

Zack spotted Sam. He wore one of his trademark vulgar Hawaiian shirts. He carried a tall umbrella drink in one hand, a plate full of food in the other.

"Sammy, baby! I didn't expect to see you here."

"Yes, well, wonders never cease."

Zack poked his head around her, eyeballing Phil up and down.

"Who's your curious-looking friend?"

"Zackster, hey, this is my friend… Keats. Keats, this fun guy is Zack, the voice of the toaster."

Zack smiled and sucked on his straw.

"A pleasure," said Phil. "I'd shake your hand, but I have a painting to deliver to a... Mr. Adams."

"Cool, dude. You bought Dan a painting? C'mon, then." He leaned toward Sam. "I've been dabbling in art collecting myself."

Sam and Phil followed behind Zack. The living room was massive, with high ceilings. Sam gazed at all the modern furniture, which completely conflicted with the architectural style of the house. Dan sat on one end of a sweeping white leather sofa, surrounded by beautiful people.

Moon, blues legend, sat stoically on the opposite end, wearing his signature hat and sunglasses. Sam did a double-take. She knew Moon was about seventy-two, and a couple of times when she'd picked Kyle up after school for Peter, Kyle had plugged his iPhone into her stereo and Moon had been his main playlist. For a rich, white kid, Kyle sure seemed to "get" Moon's music.

Dan sat, looking completely disengaged between ridiculously beautiful women. One, Sam was positive, was a Victoria's Secrets Angel. Another she recognized from a makeup campaign. Both their faces held completely vapid gazes.

Dan's eyes lit up when he saw Zack approaching with Sam and Phil. He immediately jumped up from the couch.

"Excuse me, ladies."

He pushed his way through more beautiful people, puffing out his former pro athlete chest when he reached Sam. She felt the heat as she was certain he was undressing her with his eyes.

"God, you look beautiful, Samantha."

*Oh, now I'm Samantha. This is definitely going to be the full-court press.*

Dan glanced at Phil. Sam could see his eyes registering Phil's bizarre yellow glasses and ridiculous hair.

"So this is the guy? This is the artist?"

"Yes, this is Keats. Um, Keats, this is Dan, the man who won the auction for your latest painting."

Phil lowered the painting from above his head, holding it by his side, and extended his hand.

"Pleased to meet you, Dan. And thank you for noticing my work."

"My pleasure… Keats was it?"

"Yes, just Keats."

"Well," Dan looked intently at Sam. "As a collector, I can't wait to see it!"

Phil handed Dan the painting. Dan looked around at the crowd. Many of the beautiful people had stopped talking and were looking on with curiosity.

Dan held the canvas up and looked at it. It was prominently signed "KEATS."

"This is… incredible!"

Sam tried to keep her face impassive.

Dan turned his head and looked to the crowd. Bewildered faces instantly shift to phony smiles. He turned back to Phil.

"I love it, Mr. Keats. I've made a spot for it right over here."

"Dan, it's Keats. Just Keats." He pushed his yellow glasses up his nose slightly.

"Yes, of course."

Dan walked over to a wall where a space waited, a light already in place to illuminate his latest masterpiece. He hung the canvas, backed away, folded his arms across his chest and stared at it.

After leaning in, stepping back, and making a show of taking in the painting, he turned to face his guests. Sam saw several registering confusion. *Yeah, I'd be confused to. Because this painting is really, horribly atrocious. He'd be better off with a velvet Elvis or a painting of dogs playing poker.*

"It's quite something, isn't it?" Dan asked.

An older guy, wafting cologne, in a black silk T-shirt, expensively tailored pants, and what Sam guessed were the latest Gucci loafers, strolled over self-importantly.

"So, Mr. Keats, I see that the negative space is quite prominent. May I ask… what was your intent?"

People gathered around, fascinated. Sam felt like she wanted to throw up. She was certain this was the moment when she would have to call Peter and say, "Show's over. The crazy train has derailed."

Instead, Phil said, "Yes, well, that was the driver in this *particular* piece. It literally *dragged* me in that direction. I found myself… *floating*… in uncertainty."

The "critic" stroked his chin and offered the slightest of nods. "I see." He stepped back and stared at the painting. "And has anyone mentioned that the iconicity of the negative space verges on codifying the montage elements?"

"Indeed!" Phil enthused. "I have heard that… a few times. But honestly, I think it's the disjunctive perturbation of the biomorphic forms that *heightens* the *simplicity* of the exploration of montage elements."

Sam scrunched her face, standing in awe. *WTF? Where is he even coming up with this shit?*

Dan hesitated, wrinkled his brow before turning back to the painting, fingers over his closed mouth. *Hmm.*

Another impossibly thin, breezy blonde with an airbrushed tan and glitter on her chest walked up and stroked Dan's back. "It's absolutely stunning!"

Suddenly, like a hurricane tide bursting through a sandbagged wall the room began buzzing.

"It's amazing, Dan."

"What an eye you have."

"A brilliant discovery!"

"How did you find him?!"

Zack stared at the painting, puzzled. He slurped an oyster from its shell. He swallowed, wiped his mouth with the back of his hand, and said, "Looks like someone threw a rag at it."

Everyone nearby froze in disbelief. Horrified eyes turned on Zack.

Phil turned slightly, caught Zack's eye, and winked.

Dan rolled his eyes and ignored Zack's comment, continuing to stare at the painting. "Yes... the... negative space does codify the montage elements. I see it now!"

Sam wanted to smash the painting and run from the room. *Sure, you see it now.*

Dan turned to the pretentious crowd. "The other fascinating aspect is how Keats *showcases* his work. You can watch them come to life right before your eyes. And... you *bid* on them *while* they're being painted! How novel is *that*?! He is literally changing our relationship with art."

Phil looked around, hands on hips, a smug smile on his lips. Sam placed her hand on his shoulder. "If anyone's interested in viewing his work, or bidding on one, just go to I AM KEATS DOT COM. His site crashed from all of the recent activity, but it should be back up shortly."

Dan looked at Sam and smiled, then turned to the crowd.

"Yes, by all means go. Enjoy the show. But ultimately... you'll be wasting your time."

Sam's eyes widened.

He winked at her. "You'll be bidding against Big Dan."

Dan pulled Phil over to him and clapped him on the back. "Keats, I want to introduce you to a friend of mine."

He brought him over to Moon, who was sitting quiet and cool. Sam trailed behind them.

"Hey Moon, I want you to meet the artist Keats. My latest discovery."

Moon nodded at Phil, turned slowly, and looked up at Phil's painting.

Phil and Dan waited patiently for Moon's reaction.

Moon spoke flatly, but with an enticing southern drawl. "I was driving through Memphis... 1956?... 57?... It was late... after a gig... when out of *nowhere*! Somethin' steps out in the road."

The crowd was mesmerized.

"I swerved man, but... I don't know. There was a loud... badump badump!" He raised his hands, which Sam noticed had long fingers, wrinkled yet she knew he played like someone fifty years younger.

Moon continued. "Anyways, I pull over and walk back a bit and I see this flattened... somethin' in the road."

Moon looked back up at the painting. "It kinda looked like that."

A pretentious-looking woman stepped alongside Sam and glared at Sam's skirt. "Oh honey, is that a Mark Eisen?"

"Oh no." Sam grinned. "It's a Mar... Shals."

"I don't believe I know him."

Zack had wandered over, and stood nearby, slurping another oyster, as usual a confused expression on his face.

"I think he's... Moroccan."

After suffering through tours of the insufferable, Sam steered Phil out of Dan's house and to her Jeep. Everyone at the party was monopolizing Phil—wanting to take selfies with Keats.

As Sam drove the Jeep, stars above them, Phil passed out. He was several sheets to the wind, and seemed to be partial to tequila shots out of one model's belly button.

Once back at Phil's place, Sam poked him.

"Keats! We're here!"

Phil slowly opened his eyes, looking straight ahead. The night breeze blew through the open-sided Jeep.

"O-kaaaay then. I guess this is it," Phil said, his voice slurring slightly. "I gotta tell ya, that was... fun."

"Yeah, it really was." She smiled.

Phil reached for his nonexistent door. He whipped his head to the right. Then whipped back to look at Sam.

"OK, I don't wanna alarm you or anything… but I think someone stole your doors."

Sam laughed. "Good night, Phil. Um. Keats. It was certainly an experience."

Phil turned, swung his right leg out of the Jeep and got jerked back by the seat belt. Sam shook her head, reached over, and poked the seat belt release button. Phil ejected and tumbled out, landing in some bushes.

"Oh my God! Are you OK!?" She laughed when he raised a thumbs-up.

"Well, hello there Mr…. Bush. You know, I don't think I voted for you. But, I'm not really sure."

He staggered to his feet. He patted the bush. "I'm good, I'm good."

She laughed again. "Well, Keats? There's ya déjà vu!"

Phil made a foot over foot, sideways jaunt to his door. Looking back at Sam, he saluted her good night.

Sam pulled away and headed toward home. "Well, Peter," she whispered to the night-time sky. "Your plan is definitely not going according to plan."

~

*Keats.*

*He was a character all right.*

*So my uncle was now wearing glasses like Elton John, painting while half-naked, and shaving lightning bolts into his head.*

*I am pretty sure—in fact, I am one hundred percent sure—that this Keats guy was not what my dad had in mind when he came up with this whole crazy idea.*

*Dad wanted Uncle Phil to come into his destiny—a destiny my dad believed was far greater, more important, more brilliant than the life Uncle Phil had been living. All it would take was a nudge. A little push. Just tweak this a little and Uncle Phil would have a whole new story.*

*It would be as easy as climbing on a bicycle and peddling. Only our trip should have shown him that it's never as easy as that. Just like the crash Uncle Phil sustained, there were forces building—call it quantum physics, call it the fates—call it whatever you like. But like a supercollider, all of the atoms in this particular* experiment were under pressure. They were swirling and spinning.

And it wouldn't take more than the flick of a lighter to watch it all explode.

# Waiting for the Spark

*ome people are destined to be Atlas. This is what I learned. Friday after school I asked Ramona about my Dad and Uncle Phil. My dad was staying late at the office (big shock!) and couldn't drive me home. Ramona pulled up to the car pool lane.*

*"Hello, mi cielito." She grinned as I slid into the passenger seat.*

*"Hey, Tia Ramona." I pulled on my seatbelt. "Let me guess. Another late day at the office?"*

*She sighed. "You know your father—"*

*"—is a very important and busy man," I parroted one of Ramona's most common refrains.*

*She shot me a sidelong look—the stern Ramona look my dad and Uncle Phil told me about. I grinned and waggled my eyebrows at her, and then she suddenly burst into this wonderful laugh.*

*As we sat in traffic, I asked, "Why are my uncle and my dad so different? They're brothers. Same parents. Same upbringing."*

*"Oh, Kyle, isn't that such a mystery? Two boys, loved, treasured, both suffer an unthinkable loss." She was silent a moment. "And then both are loved," she laughed and winked at me. "Both are then loved next by their nanny-turned-guardian. I loved them equally. So why is your father... your father? And your Uncle Phil... uniquely your Uncle Phil?"*

*"Exactly!"*

*"Your father is Atlas. I tried to stop him from being so, but... he was already so determined."*

*"Atlas?"*

*"Destined to hold the sky on his back. Your father, after he lost his parents—your grandparents—he became a little man overnight. His face, always so serious. Always as if he had burdens no one else understood. It became his identity. Perfect Peter. That was his... story. All that loss and he chose to become perfect. To carry the sky on his back."*

*I stared out the window and kind of felt bad for my dad. I thought of all the nights I would walk past his office and see him at his computer going over financials. Once, he just sort of forgot it was me for a minute—I was maybe twelve—and he said, "All three hundred employees of the studio count on me. This studio folds and everyone from the receptionist to the writers to the animators to the CFO will be out of a job."*

*I definitely could believe his shoulders were getting heavy carrying the whole sky.*

*"And Uncle Phil?" I asked.*

*"Oh, my Phil was the dreamer. He never made plans, and from minute to minute, life with little Phil was an adventure. He left me breathless! But he just couldn't ever be disciplined about anything. He changed his major four times in college! Four times. Anyway, I don't know why they are so different—but they are brothers. And no matter what, that is true. They love each other."*

*Brothers. My dad always seemed to rush through the subject whenever I brought up Uncle Phil. I wasn't sure what was the matter. Uncle Phil could not help losing his memory. It wasn't his fault. But it was more than that. Something I still could not understand.*

*I never had a brother. Or a sister. Mom is in her "I like being alone" phase and is planning to climb Kilimanjaro this summer. And dad? Dating? Hopeless. He seems to exchange one beautiful blonde for the next, but they all leave him because he is never available. My mom once said, "And that includes emotionally." So at the rate my parents are going, I'm guessing I'll be an only child forever. And my mom has no siblings. And I don't see Uncle Phil giving me a cousin any time soon.*

*But I would have given anything for a brother.*

*That was why Jonesy was so important to me.*

⁓

Phil stumbled out of his clothes, leaving them scattered on the studio floor. He was exhausted, and drunk. *That was one hell of a coming out party.* He placed a fresh canvas on his easel, started to walk to his bedroom, and froze.

Adopting a determined look, he shuffled back, grabbed a paint-soaked cloth, and hurled it—hard—at the canvas, even winding up like a Major League pitcher.

He paused, raised his hands in front of his eyes, index fingers and thumbs extended to frame up and view his splat.

Giving a half nod of satisfaction, he wiped his hands on his briefs, then wobbled his way into his bedroom.

Peter sat at his kitchen counter, laptop open, papers spread out. His housekeeper, Lan, wiped around him, tsk-tsking him. She hated that he worked in the kitchen. She was always Feng-Shui-ing him, moving a plant here, a vase there, the chair over here. Lan, especially, hated clutter.

"Lan," he knew he was starting a useless argument, because it had been the same one since he hired her when he got divorced. "You gotta start placing the appliances back where you find them. I'm trying to maintain a certain workflow here."

She turned and gave him an over-the-shoulder, "whatever" glance. "Workflow does not belong in kitchen. You have a very big office, Mr. Peter."

She walked away, and he shook his head. He was always losing battles in his own house. Speaking of which: "Kyle!"

Kyle's voice shouted down from the second floor. "Yeah, Dad?"

"Remember, you're not leaving this house until your homework is done."

Peter punched a button on his laptop. On the screen, Phil's new website popped up, prominently displaying: I AM KEATS!

Peter rolled his eyes and clicked the live stream/auction link to check the bidding… WTF?! He lurched back, almost falling off of his chair.

The bids were skyrocketing! Tens of thousands of dollars. How had anyone even found the site?

He clicked on the painting. It looked like a giant splotch. Like what the *hell* was that?

Dan pulled on his bathrobe, a blonde from the night before occupying the other side of the bed.

He picked up his iPhone and checked his messages. He had about twenty texts from people who had gone to his party, all texting pretty much the same thing: CHECK OUT KEATS!

Dan padded into the bathroom and pressed on the flat-screen panel on the wall, pulling up the Internet.

"Holy shit!" he exclaimed when he saw the climbing prices.

"What is it, baby?" The blonde called to him from the bedroom.

"Nothing, babe. Just that Big Dan knows how to pick 'em."

"Of course you do!"

Dan rolled his eyes. "Listen, I've got a meeting downstairs in about ten minutes. You understand, right?"

"Sure, baby."

He brushed his teeth, ran water through his hair, then went downstairs to meet his long-time financial adviser just as the bell rang.

"Hey, Marvin!" Dan greeted him as he opened the door.

He showed the older man into the massive great room, gesturing to the couch. Dan sat in a leather chair, still in his robe. He grabbed a cigar from the humidor and snipped the end and lit it, smoking like a chimney. He knew he still looked very, very rough. He couldn't remember much past his fifth Presidential Select bourbon, and he groaned a little, realizing he probably single-handedly consumed $700 of the expensive whiskey.

Marvin, dressed in plaid pants and a plum dress shirt, looked around the room, pausing to squint at the new painting on the wall, but then shook his head and clasped his hands, leaning back a moment.

"I called for this meeting because you need to get serious here, Dan. Do you have any idea how bad things are?"

Dan blew a huge puff of cigar. "No, Marvin. I don't know. My credit's still A+."

"That's part of the problem. You think all you have to do is sign your name and somehow that means everything's good."

Marvin unclasped his hands and leaned forward. "Listen closely. You-are-spending-way-more-than-you-are-taking-in! Capisce?"

Dan put his cigar into a Waterford ashtray. "The restaurants—"

"—are hemorrhaging money. Grilled cheese sandwiches aren't the hot new thing anymore." Marvin looked thoughtful. "The one, potentially viable investment is that studio… Apollo, and their new… 'toaster' movie. *My God, did I just say that?* And frankly, that's a crapshoot… or moonshot. Pick a metaphor."

Dan's eyes narrowed. "Funny guy. Let's not forget who got me into that fucking crapshoot."

"I didn't get you into a god-damn thing. I brought you an investment opportunity. You risked far more than I advised. Over what, a woman?"

Dan exhaled sharply.

"Anyway, that's irrelevant. As of now, you're still on course to double your investment. But… that depends on the project. And the way it's going, there's a real chance you'll be making single digits."

"Well, maybe it's time we play hardball... renegotiate. Get us a piece of the merch."

Marvin shook his head. "We've been over this. That's *never* been an option."

"Yeah, well guess what? I didn't expect to be losing money. That's never been an 'option' either."

"You knew it was a gamble. That's investing. Sometimes you win, sometimes you lose."

"Well Marv, that's where you're wrong. Big Dan doesn't lose."

A clicking of heels down the staircase made Dan turn his head. The blonde was teetering down the stairs in her party outfit, smudges of mascara under her eyes.

She sauntered over to Dan, bent over, exposing her cleavage, and gave him a kiss on the lips. "You were amazing last night..." She giggled. "*Big* Dan."

"So were you... Amber—"

"It's Angela."

"Right. So were you Angela. Sorry. Didn't get much sleep—thanks to a certain someone." He winked at her. "Yes... so Angela. I'm talking business right now, baby. I'll call you later. OK?"

She turned to leave, and Dan slapped her ass. She giggled again before clicking away perched on her five-inch gold stilettos.

Marvin shook his head. "Look, do what you want. You always do anyway. But in the meantime, it's my job to try and right this ship. So reel in the spending, or you *will* go under. No more parties with caterers and top-shelf booze every weekend."

"Marv, my man, don't worry, I got it handled."

Marvin pointed to Dan's new Keats painting on the wall. "No. You clearly don't. Like that… whateverthefuckitis? What'd you pay for *that*?"

"Nice, huh? And not that it's *really* any of your business… but… ten."

Marvin rolled his eyes. "I thought the whole grilled cheese thing was god-damn weird—"

"What?!"

"Look, this is what I'm talkin' about. You can't be spending money on shit like that."

"Yeah, well we'll see if Big Dan made a wise decision on that… *whateverthefuckitis*."

Marvin stood and walked towards the door. "It's always an adventure, Dan. Like I said, do whatever the hell you wanna do. I'll talk to you later."

Dan watched Marvin leave, then turned and looked up at Phil's painting. *Marv doesn't know that Keats is becoming more famous by the moment.*

He stared at it in deep thought.

⁓

Monday morning after the party, Dan strolled in to the studio and walked up to Sam at her desk, flashing his obscenely white smile.

"Oh, hey Dan, how are you?"

"Better now, baby. Now that I see your beautiful smile. How are you?"

"I'm good, thanks." She finished on her keyboard and turned to face him more fully. "And thanks again for buying my friend's painting. Since your party, he's been getting a ton of traffic on his site. It's crazy!"

"Glad to help. First of all, that makes my painting worth more. And I told you... Big Dan has an eye for talent." He leaned down and winked at her. "— and for beauty."

Sam tried to hide how uncomfortable he made her feel. "Peter should be right with you."

"I'm in no hurry. So when are you gonna grace me with your presence and accompany me to dinner?"

Peter's door opened. Sam turned to Peter, relieved.

"Finally." She returned her gaze to Dan. "Sorry he kept you waiting."

Dan turned and spied Peter and Phil walking out of Peter's office.

"Hey, Keats!" He looked confused. "What are *you* doing here?"

"Oh, hey Dan. Great party the other night. You didn't know Pete's my brother?"

"Um, no, I did not."

Dan glanced at Sam, offering a questioning eye.

Peter strode forward. "How you doing, Dan?"

Dan furrowed his brow. "Oh, you know, life is good. You ready to go over those numbers?"

"Absolutely."

Peter and Dan walked past Phil and into Peter's office. Dan turned and watched Phil walk over to Sam.

"Wow. I'm in shock. Why didn't anyone tell me Keats was your brother?"

"I didn't realize you didn't know——" Peter was *not* looking forward to hashing out who Keats really was.

Dan looked at Peter hostilely. "Were you guys trying to pull somethin' over on me?"

Peter was irked. He had heard about what Dan did—bidding over Sam's shoulder like the show-off he was. "What the hell are you talkin' about?!"

"I just find it *really* strange that Sam never mentioned it."

He paced. "That day I came in, and she was on his website, was that some kind of... set-up or somethin'? Knowing if I bought his painting, I could make him into something?"

Peter seethed. "I have no idea what you're talking about, but I know I don't like it——"

Dan seemed to sense he was making Peter furious. "OK, forget it." He put up his hands. "So, how are things looking?"

"Fine."

"Ya know..." Dan turned to face him. "I was talking to Marv and he thinks we should renegotiate. Take a look at the merchandizing."

"Marvin suggested that?" Peter knew Marvin as a straight shooter.

"Yeah, but I told him that you and I had a deal." Dan raised an eyebrow. "However, he does have a point. With everything I have ridin' on this, it would be nice to know that... things were moving in the right direction."

"Things *are* moving in the right direction. It's just taking longer than expected. And just so you know, I'm actively looking for additional investors. So, if you know anyone... that could help."

"OK, I'll give it some thought."

Peter hated shaking the money tree. He wished he could just focus on the stories, on the art. For a brief moment, he wished he could be Keats, making art, instead of dealing with investors, producers, and moneymen—and women.

"So here's where we're at..." Peter gestured at a large drawing board table with storyboards and sketches strewn all over it. He opened his laptop to show Dan some of the early animation.

Dan walked over, standing behind Peter, leaning over his shoulder, one hand on Peter's desk, the other on his own hip.

"We've cut back on the number of characters. So that should speed things up significantly."

Peter clicked on an Excel spreadsheet. Dan looked down at the document, then turned and drilled distrustful, manipulating eyes into the side of Peter's head.

～

*I keep wondering where and when I would possibly use pre-calc in life. Now, I know if I ask my math teacher, he will tell me a million ways we use math in real life. And I know if I talk to my music teacher, Mr. Rhimes, he'll tell me that music and math have more than a passing acquaintance.*

*Okay, but chemistry? I will just say this: You have to wear those ridiculous, dorky safety glasses in my school. And there is no arguing about it. Miss Mooney is like this insane stickler for the rules. She tells everyone that "two elements could be combustible."*

*And this is supposed to justify looking like a complete ass in front of all of my classmates. Goggles over my glasses. And mine don't fit right. So I look like even more of an idiot.*

*But I digress.*

*I realize that I should—in a college entry essay—say how much I love school and that I am so motivated. But I'll be honest: chemistry and I are not friends. But, I do know this. I do not have to have an A+ in chemistry (you have my transcripts, so you already know I have a B+) to deduce that my dad was under a whole lot of stress. And that Uncle Phil's success was getting to him.*

*Because Keats was getting to him.*

*Are you sitting down? Of course, you probably are. You're reading my application essay. Well, here's the scoop. Uncle Phil was becoming a phenomenon. His website was going viral. People were bidding tens of thousands of dollars for his crazy paintings.*

*It started after the party Keats and Sam went to. You can bet every single one of those celebrity-loving sycophants (I am hoping I am impressing you with an SAT word!) logged onto their computers on Saturday morning and bid, bid, and bid. But you know how it is with people who love being... you know, the cultured people. The important people. The ones in the know. They told other people. Who told others, and so on, and so on.*

*And before you knew it, Uncle Phil, aka Keats, was raking in the money. He got a new car, custom plates... new wardrobe. He was even mentioned in gossip columns—"famous performance-artist Keats."*

*And none of this was making Dad happy. I mean, it should have been, but things were getting weirder by the day.*

So I really did not need my chemistry teacher confirming to me—we were headed toward combustion.

And just so I'm clear, I don't mean in a good way.

# Peter's Creation

 *ho are you?*
*What labels do you own?*
*Professor.*

*Actor.*

*Teacher.*

*School psychologist.*

*Doctor.*

*Admissions counselor.*

*I think we all wear some labels we think we own. And we don't own the labels that maybe we should.*

*So Uncle Phil—Keats—was adopting a role of famous painter. Rich painter. No more crappy apartment for him! But none of it was making any sense to Dad. How does someone wake up one day as a famous painter? But that's the world of crazy, unintended consequences.*

*And if you're thinking it was all my dad's idea, you're sort of right.*

*But is that all it takes? Changing some memories around?*

*Is it that easy?*

*No. It was like Dad wrote a script for how he thought this was all going to go. And then a bolt of lightning hit the script, set it on fire, someone hosed it with a fire extinguisher, and now the pieces were just scraps of ash.*

*Maybe it was all turning out for the best, but I can tell you as sure as my name is Kyle David Anderson, this transformation was not making Dad happy.*

*He felt like he had created a monster, and it was on the loose.*

⁓

Peter rolled up into his driveway, pulling his car next to Phil's brand-new, black-on-black Ferrari. He exhaled and gripped the steering wheel.

Briefcase in hand, he exited, stopped, zeroed in on Phil's vanity license plate, and rolled his eyes. *Are you kidding me?*

KEAT$

He walked into the kitchen. It looked like rabid wolves had made sandwiches on Peter's kitchen counter—crumbs and an open jar of pickles, spilled something or other.

*Phil has always been a pig. And where the hell is Lan?*

He opened the fridge. He grabbed a perfectly made plate of a sandwich on focaccia bread and a scoop of potato salad that Lan had left for him. He noticed that Phil—Kyle would never be so disrespectful—had left a spoon sticking in the bowl of potato salad.

He could hear music *blasting* upstairs, this blues crap Kyle had taken an interest in. Like he couldn't listen to music from *this* millennium. And how could he study with that racket?

"Kyle!" He shouted at the ceiling.

Kyle sat at his desk, trying to study. Blues music blared from floor speakers.

Phil wandered around the room, meddling, touching everything. Kyle glanced over his shoulder and saw his uncle pick up his Moon hat from Jonsey, try it on in the mirror, and then place it back on the hook on the wall before moving on to a bunch of origami paper cranes his friend Ellie made for him.

Phil suddenly dropped to his knees and pulled out Kyle's guitar from under the bed. He opened the case and gave a soft whistle at the Ibanez, polished to a sheen. He pulled it out and began to play air guitar with it to the time of the music. He grabbed a pair of sunglasses off Kyle's dresser and put them on.

Kyle snorted a laugh. He had never known an adult to act like a kid. His dad couldn't relax for five minutes. Even their vacations were built around "achieving" something—climbing a mountain, that stupid bike trip when Uncle Phil got hurt, scuba lessons and then reef diving. But his dad wouldn't do karaoke the time they went to Japan, or even the wave when they went to the occasional NFL game.

Kyle put down his pencil and gave up on the studying and instead watched his uncle continue to "play" his guitar. Finally, Phil dropped the guitar on the bed, walked over to the window, fiddled with the shade and revealed Moon. He stepped back.

"Hey! I *know* that guy!"

"In real life?" Kyle was sure his uncle was joking.

"Yup!"

"Are you kidding me? I own everything he's ever done!"

"Yeah, that's Moon. I've been spending more time with this whole cool crowd, this guy Dan—"

"Not that 'Big Dan' guy? The one who always speaks about himself in third person and who's always chasing Sam?"

"The very one. And anyway, there's Moon, this other guy Louie—"

"Moon's bass player?" Kyle couldn't believe what he was hearing.

"Yeah. Man, you really know your Moon stuff. You wanna meet 'im?"

"Oh my, God! Are you being serious right now?!"

Phil turned down the volume on the music. "Yeah, there's a party Friday night. He's gonna be there."

Phil pointed at the shade. "Why's that poster pasted on there like that?"

"So I can close it so my dad won't see it."

Phil's eyes widened. "Really? How come?"

"He thinks my music is a—" Kyle lifted his hands and did "air quotes." "—frivolous distraction."

Phil sat down on the edge of the bed, hands folded in front of him. His expression became serious. "Kyle, look, I'm gonna let you in on a little secret. Well, actually, it's a humongous secret."

Kyle swallowed.

Phil, looking at Kyle directly in his eyes, said, "You, me, your mom, your dad, your friends, your teachers... we all have one thing in common. You know what that is?"

Kyle shrugged. "Um. We're all human."

"True, and as humans, we all want to be happy. Heck, we even put it in the Constitution: life, liberty, *and*... show me how smart you are, brilliant nephew, I don't remember."

"Pursuit of happiness."

"Right, and do you know what the greatest barrier to happiness is?"

Kyle thought of his mom. In addition to her climb to Kilimanjaro, she was immersed in Eastern philosophies, her house an oasis of orchids, water fountains, Buddha statues, Quan Yin statues, Ganesh statues.

"Buddha said it's desire," Kyle offered.

"Bullshit, Grasshopper. It's when we *suppress* our desires, our dreams... to please everyone but ourselves."

Kyle furrowed his brow.

Phil picked up the guitar. "It's craving Kyle, for some outcome... Believing that the world, something other than yourself, is the source of your happiness.

That's what'll eat you up. Like do you play the guitar for the sheer expressive joy of it, for what it feeds your soul, or do you play anticipating an unseen audience waiting to *judge* whether you are 'good enough'? Let's suppose someone takes up writing, and they love it! They get so jazzed from writing. But do they quit writing because a voice inside them—some story they've been fed, or they've made up themselves—says they'll never be as good as Hemingway so what's the point?"

"Lots of kids at my school have already given up stuff they love to do because there are better clubs or things to do that look better to colleges on your application. Like there's a robotics club, and most of the kids in it are doing it to look good for college. The kid who started it—Henry—he loves it. Like one day he's going to work for SpaceX or Blue Origin, I promise you. But he and a couple of others are the only ones. The rest do it to pad their applications."

"That's not living. That's not following your passion. Listen to me, Grasshopper, because aside from the Birds and Bees talk you probably got from your mom or dad, this may be the most important. Don't expect a *thing* from anyone, including yourself.

Just do what *you* love to do... every day. Be loose and light and let life take you for a ride. Dig?!"

From downstairs, Kyle could hear his dad screaming for him again: "Kyle!"

He really wanted to talk to his Uncle Phil more. Every other adult in his life asked him questions like they all had an Almost-Adult Checklist:

*Have you taken your SAT's yet?*

*What was your score?*

*Where are you thinking of applying?*

*What major are you thinking of?*

And on and on. No one talked to him about what he loved to do.

He guessed that Uncle Phil saw the disappointed look on his face.

"Go ahead, my favorite nephew. I really have to urinate."

"Aren't I your only nephew?"

"That's what they tell me!"

Kyle laughed and hustled out of the room.

Phil wandered into Peter's bedroom and snooped around. *Who is this Peter guy, really?* He looked at the giant toaster painting above the bed and rolled his eyes. He sneaked a look at Peter's closet.

"Holy crap," he whispered under his breath. "There must be ten-thousand dollars of just *suits* in here. And how many Gucci loafers can one man own? You can only wear one pair a time."

He walked over to Peter's drafting table and the unfinished children's book. Flipping to the front, he saw the name: BY MARK JAMES ANDERSON

Phil flipped through, stopped at a scene, picked up a pencil, and scrawled something.

Kyle walked into the kitchen. Peter shook his head. *Finally.* "What's with the loud music? Aren't you supposed to be studying for your SATs? And doing that homework assignment for chemistry?"

"I know all about combustion. Believe me."

"Sure. You think you know it all. So did I when I was your age."

Phil walked down the stairs. "Hey, bro. Kyle and I were just catchin' up."

"Uh-huh. How long have *you* been here?"

Phil looked at Kyle and shrugged. Kyle visibly tensed.

"I dunno. An hour maybe?"

Peter clenched his jaw. "An hour. So, Kyle, have you studied since you got home?"

"A little. I was gonna—"

Peter cut him off. "I suggest you get back to it."

Kyle rolled his eyes.

"Bye, Uncle Phil. I mean..." He grinned. "Uncle... Keats."

"See ya, Kyle. I'll touch base later about Friday."

He winked at Kyle, who broke into an even wider grin and raced upstairs.

Peter narrowed his eyes. "What's going on Friday, Uncle... *Keats*?"

"Uncle-nephew stuff."

"Oh yeah?" He grit his teeth. "Look, stay away from him. He's on a great path."

"Path? Meaning?" Phil crossed his arms.

Looking at his brother closely, Peter could see he had pierced his ear. *Really? What the hell was next?*

"Meaning, *Keats*, don't distract him."

"Distract him? I'm trying to *encourage* him."

"To do what? Be like you?"

Phil looked confused. Then his face became serene. "What's wrong with being like me? I'm not doing too bad. Doing what I love. Movin' on up! Have you checked out my new wheels? Livin' the dream, bay-be. Livin' the dream."

"It's a dream all right."

"What's that supposed to mean?"

"Nothin', just stay the hell away from Kyle. Don't confuse him with your bullshit."

Phil stared at his brother. "You know…" He paused as a smirk twisted the corners of his mouth. "I thought of a perfect metaphor for you."

"Really?"

"Yeah, you're like a serial killer."

Peter closed the lid of his laptop, sat up taller, and affected being interested in his brother's bullshit. In his most sarcastic voice, he said, "Fascinating theory, there Keats. Uh-huh, I'm *dying* to hear this one."

"'Dying' to hear it? You're so fucking clever."

Peter rolled his eyes.

"Did you ever see those shows where they profile serial killers, and they end up linking all the murders to the fact that the killer hated his mother and so he went out and found women who reminded him of her and *symbolically* killed her over and over again? Meanwhile the sicko and his dear ol' mom enjoy Sunday dinner together, every week? I mean, damn, why not just kill the bitch and get it over with, right?"

"Kill the mother," Peter uttered incredulously. Maybe his brother's head injury was worse than Dr. Singh initially thought.

"Yes. Leave those innocent women alone to live their lives."

Peter stared at Phil with amazement.

"What the *fuck* are you talking about?"

"You! You basically hate your life. You wander through it like a damn zombie. Since I left the hospital, I never—and I mean *never*—have seen you spontaneously smile, laugh, act for a moment in some way as if you are actually *enjoying* this life, this amazing life you have. So you're *symbolically* fixing it by trying to control everyone else's lives. Micromanaging. Don't you see? It's kind of like life improvement by proxy."

"Are you through?" Peter said in a flat monotone.

"As a matter of fact, I'm pretty sure I am."

Phil walked over, grabbed Peter's sandwich, and took a bite. Peter was about to knock the sandwich out of his brother's hand when Lan walked in.

She had several expensive suits and dress shirts draped over her arm.

"I go to cleaners now."

"Yeah, OK, but listen…" Peter reached up and stroked his collar. "Tell your buddy, one more time, more starch on the shirts."

Phil chewed on the sandwich, then talked with his mouth full. "Riiight. 'Cause you ain't stiff enough."

The housekeeper turned to Phil and smiled.

Phil then shocked her by speaking Chinese. "Dàn yexu bùshì? Wo hái méiyou jiànguò ta yu yigè nurén hen zhang yiduàn shíjian." *"But maybe not? I haven't seen him with a woman for a long time."*

Lan stared at Phil. Her upper lip trembled, and then she doubled over in uncontrollable laughter. Finally, she straightened up and walked out the door, shaking her head, laughing, mumbling to herself in her native tongue.

"What the *hell* was that, Keats?"

"Huh?" Phil looked at him guilelessly.

"You speak *Chinese*?!"

Phil smirked. "I didn't realize it. I guess I do!"

And with that, Phil took Peter's sandwich and marched out the door, whistling a tune.

⁀

*Later that night, I plugged into my Ibanez and thought about all the things Uncle Phil had said. I put on my headphones—it was rigged so that I could practice all I wanted and my dad couldn't hear a thing.*

*I started with some Robert Cray, then some Buddy Guy. And then finally, I took on what I consider to be my personal Mount Everest. Blues for Alice by the late, great, tormented Charlie Parker.*

*I got lost in it. I tried not to think about how fast my fingers were moving across the strings, and instead to feel it all. To stop my inner critic—that Coleridge voice that told me I was just a white boy from Cali—and instead not care one bit about anything but the notes.*

*When I was done, I sat there, out of breath, and as high as my friend Cam is after he smokes weed. (I haven't even tried it—music is my high.)*

*And then I thought about something.*

*Charlie Parker was an addict. And I am not talking about a guy who maybe had a bit of a problem with alcohol or a little drugs. I am talking about hardcore heroin use, to where, at the end of his life, he was pretty much broke and homeless.*

*But Parker was amazing. They said the drugs made him unreliable—but also somehow they meant this was a man who played the saxophone like some sort of spiritual epiphany, transcending this world. People who heard him play live said it was like he was superhuman.*

*So here's the crazy thing. Because Parker was so amazing, a god among musical gods, people who admired him thought that the only way to achieve that greatness was to use drugs, to lose your inhibitions with heroin. And somehow drugs and jazz musicians became synonymous.*

*Not that I ever would have done drugs, but now that I had my talk with Uncle Phil, I had a whole new idea of music. Believe me—I want to get into your conservatory—but I now know that it is about playing from the heart. About not copying anyone! I didn't need to play like anyone else.*

*Just play like me. Kyle Anderson.*

*And with heart.*

# Heroes

*ho is your hero/heroine—and why?*

*Friday night, Uncle Phil arranged for me to meet Moon.*

*I didn't know what to wear. Think. Speak. Or feel.*

*Like, imagine you are six, and somehow you meet a guy in an Iron Man costume. You'd think that'd be pretty awesome, right?*

*I was about to come face to face with my idol.*

*And pretty much? I didn't know whether to bow to the king... or throw up.*

⁓

Phil careened towards Dan's house in his Ferrari, swerving close to parked cars, then badump...

badump... up over the sidewalk, coming to rest on Dan's front lawn.

Kyle had slid against the passenger door after Phil's horrible driving. He righted himself and smoothed his hair, then he and Uncle Phil climbed out.

Phil put his hand on Kyle's shoulder. "Relax. They're just a bunch of talkin' apes. Like you and me."

"Like you, maybe. I mean, they're famous. Me, not so much."

Phil said softly, "Famous." He shook his head. "They got some lucky breaks. So what? Anyway, at the end of the game the king and pawn go back in the same box. Remember that, my boy."

A parking valet sprinted towards them. Phil handed off a hundred. The valet grabbed it without breaking stride.

"Thanks, Keats!"

Kyle, wide-eyed, glanced back at the valet and Phil's car. He'd been to parties with his dad before—not that many since his dad was more of a "power lunch/power dinner" guy—but his dad would no-way slip a hundred to anyone.

Too wasteful.

But as he watched the valet hustle, he glanced over at his Uncle Phil. He had just made someone's day.

Phil and Kyle strolled up the lengthy walkway, with a koi pond to the right, and into the bustling party. All eyes shifted to Phil, hands extended, "Hi. Mr. Keats." It was as if a receiving line at a wedding had formed. Around him, Kyle heard people whispering, "It's him, it's Keats. Good to see you again, Keats."

Kyle's head was spinning, literally and figuratively. He kept scanning the room, all the "beautiful people," until he finally spotted Moon, sitting coolly at his spot on the far end of the couch.

Kyle's heart skipped a beat. "There he is, that's him!" He pointed.

Phil gently moved Kyle's arm down. "Relax. He's not goin' anywhere. Lemme introduce you to the host."

Phil led Kyle over to Dan, who was standing with a beautiful model-type on either side of him. Phil extended his hand to Dan. Kyle felt out of place, even with the cool, new black blazer and white silk T-shirt his uncle had bought him at Hugo Boss on the way. The models were unbelievably gorgeous—

he recognized one from a beer commercial. He kept averting his eyes, trying *really* hard not to stare at her celebrated bosom.

"A pleasure to see you again, Dan," Phil said.

"Keats, my friend. Great to see *you*. And this handsome stud with you is?"

"This is my favorite and most-amazing nephew, Kyle. Kyle, this is Dan... Adams. One of my best customers—"

Dan leaned closer to Phil and said softly, "Patron, really. And I have something I want to discuss with you later." He shook Kyle's hand. "Pleased to meet you, Kyle. Peter's boy, right? Med-school bound. He's told me a lot about you."

Inwardly, Kyle cringed. "Yeah." *Med school. Ugh.*

"We'll be right back," Phil said. "I promised Kyle I'd introduce him to Moon. I want to catch him before he leaves."

Phil hustled Kyle over to the legendary bluesman. "Moon! How's it goin', my man?"

"Good... my man. How 'bout y'all?"

"Great! Hey, I want to introduce you to my nephew, Kyle. I'd guess he's one of your biggest fans. You've been a *huge* influence on him."

Moon stood, extending his large hand, silver rings gleaming against his dark skin, with long fingers, lined with veins, the hands of a genius.

Kyle just stared at Moon's hand.

"Nice to meet you, young man."

Kyle suddenly snapped to. He shook his idol's hand. "Yes… it is. I mean… yes, Mr. Moon."

"Keats, you and the boy come down to the club one night. My guests."

"That'd be great, Moon." Phil turned to Kyle. "Give me a minute with Moon. Go grab a soda or somethin'."

Kyle watched his uncle and Moon sit on the couch and he wandered off in search of a soda. He glanced back and saw them, still talking animatedly, and then Moon was vigorously nodding his head. He wondered what that was all about.

He milled around, watched the DJ working with his equipment out by the pool, ate some appetizers— there was a sushi station. Eventually, his Uncle Phil found him, and then started to make their way to the door to leave. It was nearing midnight, but streams of people were pouring in the door.

Dan came to say good-bye.

"Sorry we gotta head out so early," Uncle Phil said. He suddenly grabbed Kyle in a headlock. "Kyle's gettin' a bit… antsy."

Dan nodded. "Yeah, Peter's got enough on his mind right now. Anyway, get back to me on that proposal. I think this can be a big win-win."

Phil nodded. "Win-win? Or—" He held up a hand, counting off each finger. "Win-win-win… win-win?"

Dan stared at Phil, confused.

"Later, dude!" Phil sang out.

The valet brought their car, and Phil and Kyle zoomed off into the night.

The next morning, Peter was at his same old spot at the expansive kitchen counter, laptop open, papers spread out, head down. Kyle walked down around noon. In his peripheral vision, Peter could see the kid had a bedhead of hair—meaning he didn't get up early to study.

Without even looking up, Peter asked, "Where were you last night?"

"Hangin' out."

"What time'd you get in?

"I dunno. Midnight?"

Lan walked into the kitchen from a back room. Purse in hand. She walked to the back door. "Mr. Anderson... I done."

"You're done? OK, do you need something?"

She avoided his eyes as she continued walking.

"No. I done *working* for you. No more. I have to go now..."

She didn't wait for an answer from Peter and just exited leaving Peter and Kyle with their mouths agape.

⁓

At the office on Monday, Peter walked by Sam's unattended desk and saw Phil's loft streaming on the monitor. He stopped, squinted, leaned down, bringing his face about ten inches from the screen. *This can't be. What cosmic mind-fuck is going on?*

"What the hell?" he whispered aloud.

There was Lan. In Phil's studio loft. She was sweeping the floor, smiling, even, he thought... no... *Is she... dancing?*

Ramona walked by him in the office.

"What are you looking at?" she asked.

"Nothing. Where the hell's Sam?"

"I saw her walking towards the conference room with Phil."

"Phil? What's *he* doin' here?"

"I don't know mijo, but whatever it is it must be something pretty funny. They were laughing really hard."

"Oh *really*?"

Peter stormed off, not even acknowledging Ramona's smile and admonishment: "Breathe, Peter."

Peter barged into the conference room. Phil and Sam were sitting at the table, laughing uncontrollably. As soon as he walked in, Sam visibly stiffened and both tried to stifle their amusement.

Peter sat and feigned lightheartedness to Sam, while shooting Phil "a look." "Wow, sounds like there's some funny shit going on."

Sam glanced away.

"Sam, would you mind giving Phil and me a minute? Wait for me in my office. I'll be right there." Peter drilled his eyes into Phil.

Sam exchanged a look with Phil. "I'll talk to you later."

Phil nodded as Sam excused herself.

Once he was sure Sam was out the door, Peter stood up. "What the hell are you doing here? Do you think everything's a joke?"

Phil grinned and looked down.

"I'm weeks away from losing this place. I don't appreciate you coming in here pulling Sam away from her work."

Phil seemed distracted. Peter looked more closely and saw his brother's eyes were moving, and he was smirking at the zig-zagging path of a tiny ant.

Peter wanted to pound the table to make his brother pay attention. But suddenly, still without looking up, Phil said, "Take it easy, bro, I didn't mean to ruffle your feathers."

Phil stood, slowly, deliberately. He walked past Peter, almost brushing into him. As he put his hand on the metal handle of the glass door, he froze. "And by the way… it's Keats."

And with that, he was gone.

Peter exhaled. What the hell was going on? It was like everything in his *very well-ordered existence* had suddenly gone crazy.

Peter walked into his office. Sam sat facing his desk. She didn't flinch as he stalked in. Peter settled into his chair across from her. They stared at each other, an uncomfortably long pause.

Phil milled about the hall. He could hear the emotions—but not the words. And the emotions were turned up to eleven on a *Spinal Tap* dial of 10. He worried he had really gotten Sam in trouble. He sneaked a peek into Peter's office and saw him finally stand up and shout.

Sam suddenly busted out of the door, looking shaken, angry.

Phil could hear his brother's final salvo. "Just fucking do what I ask, OK?!"

Phil walked up to Sam. "Meet me out front in five," he whispered.

Sam nodded and headed toward the door.

Phil walked into Peter's office. He walked over to a bookshelf, picked up a framed photo of Kyle.

"Tough guy, huh?"

"Excuse me?"

"You proud of yourself? Driving her to tears."

"Put down that picture and get the *fuck* out of my building. I've had just about enough of you, too... Keats!"

"Happy to oblige."

Phil put the frame down and walked out of his brother's office, through the reception area, and out the front door.

Sam stood in the morning sun looking down at her tapping shoe, arms folded across her chest.

Phil offered her a half-wave. "I'm sorry. I didn't mean to get you in trouble. I—"

"Don't worry about it. Peter's just being... Peter." She shook her head. "And if I didn't really *need* this job, I'd have told him to shove it up his ass a long time ago."

"So do something different. You're smart. I mean, look what you've done for me."

"Riight. What *I've* done." She exhaled. "Look when he's not like this—when... look, I'm really not sure what happened or when. He was so different when I started. His movies were so different. They had an edge to them. Maybe success caused him to quit on himself... I dunno. Anyway, now they're safe and predictable, like him. Paint by numbers. No passion. Maybe he's afraid, or—"

"Maybe he *is*. But remember, this is *his* dream you're working on, not yours. What's *your* dream?"

Sam's eyebrows lifted. "*My* dream?"

"Yeah. What lights you up? I think I heard Peter say you once did some painting yourself."

Sam paused, then looked at him and smiled. "Yes. I paint. Nothing like *you* of course." She chuckled. "But my passion? I'd love to have my own dance studio."

"Really?"

She nodded. "When I was young, I took ballet lessons, en pointe. Then I tore my Achilles—end of dancing career. It was too much for me to even look at my dance shoes. But then years later, I took a salsa class on a date. And I realized I could *still* dance really well. Maybe not en pointe, but there were so many more dances that I could do. I've been salsa-dancing and swing-dancing ever since."

"So then do it!"

Sam smirked. "Yeah, OK, *Mr. Just Do It.* In the real world you need money to start a business and make it work. There are no guarantees… Go ask your brother."

"Ask my brother," Phil said under his breath. "That's pretty funny… There's no guarantee you'll survive your drive *home* tonight. So don't let stupid shit scare you. Not if you really want something. Live your life. It's shorter than you think."

Sam stared intently at him.

"I'm serious, Sam. Have you ever wondered: Why is *success* viewed as happiness? Why isn't *happiness* viewed as success?"

"I wish I had an answer for you."

"Anyway, I've kept you *way* too long. We don't want him to hunt you down." Phil started walking away.

Sam laughed. "Thanks Phil, that helped. Oops… I mean, Keats."

"No problem. And Sam, I'm serious. Really *think* about pursuing your dance studio."

He continued to walk, glancing back over his shoulder. "Besides, if you're not *working* for him, you two might be able to finally admit you're in love with each other."

Sam's mouth dropped open. "I—"

Phil laughed loudly. "Gotcha!"

Phil walked away, laughing. He winked one last time at Sam, who laughed and looked relieved.

The next morning, Peter sat at the head of the long conference room table. Ramona on his left, head down, frantically leafing through spreadsheets. There were no more parts of the budget they could cut. And they *still* were tweaking the storyboards. He felt like the spreadsheets were taunting him, telling him how close he was to losing everything.

Zack strode in, clad in his usual Hawaiian shirt. He walked to the bagel platter, made a plate, and sat down at the opposite end stuffing his face, scanning his shirt for dropped food.

Peter glanced down at his classic antique Longines watch. "Dan and the other investors should be here in a few."

Zack took a bite of his bagel and cream cheese. "No rush, Pete."

The conference room door swung open. Three serious-looking investors walked in, carrying coffees and... *What?! Dow's Donuts bags?!*

*Weird.* Peter forced a smile. "Hey guys. C'mon in. Help yourselves to some... *bagels*."

Zack raised a half-eaten bagel, smiled, and nodded in agreement. Stoically, the investors took seats at the table. The door swung open again. Peter turned.

Dan walked in. He was carrying a Dow's Donuts bag, too! *WTF?* And behind him... *Phil?!*

"Phil… Keats… whoever the hell you are, what are you doing here?"

"I'm your new investor, bro. Here to bail your ass out."

Peter, not knowing what to do, watched Phil take a seat next to Dan. He was dumbfounded.

Zack smiled and waved, cheeks full of food. Peter tried to regain his composure. "Everyone knows my brother Phil?" *OK, that was stupid. They all walked in here together.*

They all nodded, pretentious smiles on their faces. Except Zack, who offered a big thumbs-up!

"It's Keats. My name is Keats."

"Yes, that's right… Keats." He exhaled. "OK, so… Ramona has the new projections and—"

Phil cut him off. Peter was stunned. *No one cut him off.* "Yeah… so I was lookin' over the schedule and the revised script and… you know the toaster oven?"

Phil glanced at Zack. Zack raised his hand, smiled and waved.

Phil waved back. "Yeah… so I'm thinking that maybe if we—"

Peter felt his blood pressure rising. "Look… Keats. I'm not sure you know how this works. If you invest, you're investing in *me* and my team. So please, keep your 'creative' thoughts to yourself. OK?"

Phil ignored him, turned, and talked directly to Zack and Dan.

"So here's what I'm thinking..."

Peter suddenly felt the world drop away. He felt like he was entering an altered state of consciousness. He watched, as if in a dream, as Phil blathered on. His brother was making faces, sticking out his tongue, and laughter rocked the table around him. How had he lost control of his own meeting?

Fuck that. How had he lost control of his own *company*?

No. Worse. How had he lost control of his *life*?

Peter's head spun, when he suddenly felt a hand on his shoulder. "Peter? Peter?"

It was Sam.

"I'm sorry, but you have a call—"

"I thought I've told you not to interrupt me during these meetings!"

Sam lowered her voice. "But you told me if it had anything to do with Kyle..." She leaned down and whispered in his ear. "His school's on the phone."

Peter turned to the group. They were staring at him.

"I'm sorry, but we'll have to pick this up later. Ramona, please give everyone a copy of the financials."

Peter hurried out. *Now what?!*

⁓

Peter sat across from a stern woman, hands folded in front of her. On her desk, a sign proclaimed: "Dean of Students."

"As I have explained, Ms. Utley, I have no idea where he is. I thought he was here, like he always is."

"If he *always was*, we wouldn't be having this discussion, now would we, Mr. Anderson? You know, Kyle's really hurting himself with all of these absences."

"No, I don't know. This is the first I've heard of any 'absences.' And quite frankly, considering I am paying, oh… a good sixty-five grand a year for this supposedly top-notch prep school, it's very disheartening that I am only hearing about this now."

"This log shows that we've had more than six conversations with you this past month alone, Mr. Anderson."

She handed Peter the log. Peter scanned it, clenching his jaw. He noticed something, pointed to the log, and handed it back.

"Where'd you get this phone number?"

She turned her swivel chair to her computer and punched keys.

"Apparently, you called in… a few months ago and said to use this new number for all correspondence." She pushed her glasses up the bridge of her nose and turned back to Peter. "We tried that number several times today, and finally resorted to calling your company directly."

Peter felt his blood boiling, then suddenly he had an epiphany. "Do me a favor? Look up this website: I AM KEATS DOT COM."

She turned back to her computer and punched some keys. "Keats? Like the poet?"

"Yeah. What'd you see?"

"The site says, 'Keats is currently in a mindful mode. Hold onto your… *breeches*?'" She turned to Peter, a perplexed look on her face. "It says he'll return with a breakthrough shortly. What does any of this have to do with your son's absences?"

Peter massaged his temples. "I'm not quite sure. But I can assure you it has something to do with his crazy uncle."

He promised to check into Kyle's absences then drove back to the city. His phone rang and the word "Ramona" appeared on the screen on the dash.

"Ramona? Everything OK?"

"Is everything OK with Kyle?"

"Everything's fine. What's wrong?"

"You need to know what happened when you left."

His temples throbbed. "Go ahead."

"Marvin showed up. He had papers for everyone to sign."

"Marvin? What are you talking about? What *kind* of papers?"

"Dan and Phil bought out the other investors. They now have controlling interest of the company."

Peter felt numb. "What?"

"Dan told me to schedule a companywide meeting. He and Phil want to discuss new plans—"

Peter tried to keep from crashing his Tesla into the car in front of him in fury. In a cold, even voice, he ordered, "Don't do a thing. I'll call you later."

*Slash and burn. I once learned in social studies that you have to rotate crops. So farmers—way back in colonial days—would slash crops, burn old stalks to the ground, and let the field lay fallow for a little.*

*So a wise man (my uncle) told me that sometimes, in order to live your best life, you have to slash and burn your old life. Shake things up. Follow your passion.*

*But not every farmer wants to burn everything to the ground. And my father? He wasn't even willing to strike a match.*

*Oh, and me? I was in a lot of trouble. But more on that to come.*

# Harmony and Disharmony

*M**y mother loves to give me advice about what kind of future husband to be.*

*Remember it's not all about you.*

*Ask your partner about her day.*

*Do more than your share of housework. Take out the trash. Fold laundry. Pick up your dirty socks and put them in this invention called the hamper. Don't be a lazy ass.*

*And she once had advice about going to bed angry.*

*"People will tell you to not go to bed angry, Kyle," she once told me. "And that's bullshit." (Yeah, my mom is pretty straight-up with how she talks to me.) "Sometimes, the best thing you can do is take a time-out. Wait. Sleep on it. Remind yourself that you care about this person and*

*that if you open your mouth in anger, you cannot take those angry words back."*

*Remember how I told you Mom is Zen?*
*Yeah. Dad? Not so much.*

Peter cut the call, pounded his steering wheel, and decided enough was enough. He drove toward Phil's loft.

Peter stood outside the locked door and wiggled the doorknob.

He heard a blues song from inside the studio. He couldn't make out the words, but the guitar and bass were *jamming*. And a voice that sounded young and old at the same time was wailing about… clearly pain and loss.

Peter unlocked the door with his key, entered, and saw a motley boy band of five playing on brand-new, top-of-the-line instruments. Kyle on guitar stood facing Jonesy on drums.

"So…" Peter interrupted. "You guys wanna sing the blues?"

The keyboardist look confused. "Who's that?"

Kyle reeled around. "Shit," he whispered. "Umm… Dad?"

"Get over here!" Peter commanded.

Kyle slowly slid the guitar strap off his shoulder and gently placed his beloved Ibanez in its stand. The other boys were frozen, except for the perpetually cool Jonesy, who stood from behind his drum kit and shuffled towards the door. Peter stared him down. Jonesy stopped, turned and coolly shuffled his way back to his seat.

Kyle walked over to Peter. Suddenly, his phone rang.

Peter casually held out his hand. Kyle pulled the phone from his jeans pocket. Peter grabbed the iPhone, and punched the accept button on speaker.

Phil's voice echoed through the studio. "Kyle! The jig is up, my man. Get the hell outta there, pronto!"

Peter, fury in his veins, said evenly, "Get. In. The. Car."

⟳

After dropping Kyle off at home, Peter, feeling his pulse beating at least thirty beats higher than normal, headed to the office to deal with the whole "Keats Coup."

He pulled Ramona into his office.

"There's no way I can stay. Not with 'Big Dan,' the rich idiot who talks in third person, and Phil pulling my strings."

"What are you going to do?"

"I have no idea."

"Would it be so bad to have Phil involved? I raised you both. He is your *brother*."

"Are you kidding me? He went behind my back to buy up shares of my company. Not to mention what he pulled with Kyle. What the hell kind of bullshit are we dealing with?"

"Why do you seem so disappointed with him? He's finally successful. Isn't that what you wanted? Wasn't that all part of your *plan*?"

"No, not really. He still acts like a child."

Ramona's tanned unlined face softened. "Mijo, you should be celebrating that your brother is happy and enthusiastic about life. Would you have preferred that he become—" She hesitated.

"What? More like *me*?"

"I didn't mean—"

"Look, just forget it. I understand."

A soft rap sounded on the door.

"Yeah, c'mon in," Peter commanded.

A female employee—Leigh from storyboards—slinked in. Her face was red and blotchy with tears.

"I'm really sorry to interrupt, Mr. Anderson, but everyone's in the conference room freaking out."

Peter furrowed his brow.

"Are we going to lose our jobs?"

"Who told you that?!"

"Someone overheard Keats and Dan talking."

She knotted her hands together. "Mr. Anderson, we'll all take a pay cut. We'll work weekends. We'll do whatever YOU want us to do. We believe in you."

Peter felt his body relax a little. "Okay, Leigh. Calm down. You guys misunderstood their conversation. There's nothing to worry about. Okay?"

He looked directly in her eyes. A smile of relief softening her features.

"Oh God, thank you so much Mr. Anderson! Can I let everyone know?"

"Absolutely." He spoke with authority.

Leigh rushed from the room, as if leaving before Peter could change his mind.

Ramona folded her hands on her lap. "Looks like we'll have to resort to plan B."

"Yeah... *what* plan B?"

Peter slumped back in his chair, looked up, and sighed.

⮜

Sam sat on her couch scrolling through her playlist, trying to decide which one would help her drown out this horrible week. She walked out onto her balcony and spied Phil's Ferrari up front. "What?" she wondered.

She heard a knock on her door and walked through her condo and opened it.

"Hey, Keats. What are you doing here?"

Phil handed her an envelope and walked away.

"Wait!"

Confused, she looked down at the envelope and opened it as Phil disappeared through the elevator doors.

Sam's hands trembled. It was a check with several zeros. Sam read an attached sticky note:

*I was never afraid of failure; for I would sooner fail than not be among the greatest.*
~ *John Keats*

Sam's throat went dry. She ran back into her condo and watched from her balcony as Phil drove away.

Kyle walked into the kitchen and pulled a Red Bull out of the fridge. His father was in his usual spot staring at his laptop, tie loosened, shadow beard, a half-empty bottle of Glenlivet at his side.

His dad clicked on his laptop. Without looking up, and with his "you are in SO much trouble voice," said, "You are NOT leaving this house."

"Yeah, I know."

Red Bull in hand, Kyle headed up the stairs to his room.

WWMD

That was Kyle's new mantra. What Would Moon Do? He was a guy who was playing the blues at age eleven, sneaking into honky-tonks. Moon would do just what Kyle was about to. Kyle chugged his energy drink. Then, smiling, he adjusted the blinds, climbed out the window, sprinted toward the street, and hopped into Phil's car.

"Ready?" Uncle Phil asked.

"Ready!"

Phil gunned the engine, and they drove through the L.A. night to Zack's house.

Zack's party was a lot weirder than Dan's. Big Dan had been about the models, the expensive liquor, the DJ. But Zack's party seemed to be filled with really weird, funny guys—and women—who did all kinds of cartoon voices. The mansion had a strange, retro-kitsch decor. Kyle spied unusual lobster-themed oven mitts in the kitchen. And helium balloons—lots of them—filled the living room. Different voice actors were sucking on helium and making their already weird voices even weirder.

Uncle Phil/Keats was the big hit, though. Apparently a lot of the party guests had bought his paintings. He did shots with Zack, signed a woman's arm with Sharpie, which then started this weird line-up of people wanting him to sign their arms and backs and who-knows-what-else.

Life, Kyle decided, was strange.

After they left the party, Uncle Phil's Ferrari roared through desolate city streets.

"Look!" Phil pointed and screeched the car to a halt.

Above them, a blank billboard loomed.

Phil opened his door. "Come on!"

Kyle climbed out and followed his uncle as he half-ran, half-stumbled to the trunk, which Phil popped open. Inside were paint cans, brushes and rollers. Phil pushed some into Kyle's chest.

"Uncle Phil? What are we doing?!"

"*We're* not doing anything. *It's* doing us!"

The building under the billboard was under construction. Uncle Phil opened a security gate, and they climbed up a back stairwell to the roof.

They emerged under the night sky.

"Isn't that something," Phil said.

Kyle nodded. But then he realized his uncle wasn't talking about the night sky but a ladder leaning against the building. Phil repositioned and studied it. "It's as if this was left here by the universe. Intentionally."

"Seriously, Uncle Phil, let's go home. We're gonna get in trouble."

Phil pried open a paint can.

"Ever hear of Banksy?"

"Um… Kyle stammered. His uncle was practically running in circles. *What the hell is he looking for?* His uncle suddenly zeroed in on Kyle's shirt.

"Gimme your shirt."

"What?! No way."

"Just do it!"

Kyle hesitated. His uncle held out his hand, expectantly. Finally, Kyle realized the only way he was getting off this roof was to give up his shirt. He stripped it off, tossed it to Phil, then wrapped his arms around his naked chest, freaking out.

Phil plunged it into a paint can, turned, and flung it up at the billboard. *Splat!*

Next he grabbed a brush, soaked it in paint, and ascended the ladder.

"You know… Banksy?! The street artist?"

Phil reached the top and examined his splat. "Not too shabby!"

"Can we go now?" Kyle pleaded.

Phil smeared a stroke of paint and signed his masterpiece: KEATS

"This guy… if Banksy is a guy, 'cause I don't think anyone *really* knows… has gone from a graffiti artist… a subversive *punk*… to an international star."

Phil looked down at his nephew. "Ya know how much his paintings sell for now? Go ahead! Take a guess!"

"Please, Uncle Phil? I'm getting cold."

"Half a million a pop! And get this! This Banksy character was once named one of the most influential people in the world. Can you believe that shit?!"

"So?"

"So?! So nothing! So everything! So, you can't predict or control the future. You may make it stenciling rats on buildings; you may not."

Phil, shaky, looking wild-eyed and unstable, descended the ladder. Kyle watched, distressed. "Please be careful." He stared intently at each foot his uncle placed on each wrung as he came down.

When his uncle was back firmly on the roof, Kyle said, "And I really don't understand what your sayin'."

"I'm *sayin'*... do whatever you *feel* like doin' with your life. Do whatever turns you on, 'cause ya just... never... know."

"You mean, like my music?"

Phil looked up at his creation, hands on hips. "I think it needs some red."

"Uncle Phil, my dad's very successful. He knows what works, and he says I'd end up in a subway playing for loose change."

Phil shrugged. "Great! Who gives a shit?! If you love playin' and they love listenin'."

"But I'd be pandering."

"Pandering? For what?!" His uncle looked at him quizzically, "Look Kyle, you're only pandering if you're doin' it to please *them* instead of yourself." He pointed to his heart. "What's in here! Do you get it?"

He pointed to a paint can. "What's in there? Is that red?"

Kyle bent down, looked, and shook his head no.

"Hold on, let me think," Phil said.

Phil shut his eyes. Kyle stood helplessly looking at his uncle. After a minute of silence, Phil opened his eyes again and looked at Kyle.

"Do you understand the importance of an audience?"

"Well, um, yeah, they let you know if you're doing a good job or not?"

"Well… maybe… sometimes. But never forget, you are *not* what you think others think of you. You are uniquely you, and you should honor that. The poet Keats didn't find his audience during his short life. He probably sold less than a few hundred copies of his poetry. And neither did Van Gogh, who sold only *one* painting during his lifetime. One! But they passionately pursued their callings, and are now seen as two of the world's greatest artists."

Kyle just stared at him blankly.

"Look, when you pursue your desires, you're moved by a mysterious force. You become *consumed* by that inner experience, by that... spirit."

"I've felt it," Kyle grinned tentatively.

"It's *awesome*, isn't it? But... it's not until after you share that experience, that *gift*, that you'll truly be fulfilled. And I can assure you... THAT'S not pandering. It's an invitation for others to experience your inner experience *through* your creation. Your audience is an inextricable part of your journey. You're connected. Do you understand?"

"I think so."

"Take your dad. I guarantee he was driven to create unique and meaningful stories. But he ended up focusing on the wrong audience."

"What do you mean? What audience?"

"It happens to a lot of people. When our creations lead to, quote unquote, *success*... money, influence, fame, whatever... we attract *other* audiences. We start out with an audience who loves what we've 'created', because it touches them like it touched us. But once we've 'made it...'" He made air quotes. "We start to build a following of people who love 'us,' or, more precisely, what we can 'do' for them."

"Yeah, my dad's surrounded by them."

"Yeah, it's the nature of things. People discover the transformative beauty of the ocean… and trust me, if the waves could talk they'd be happy. But then others move in and exploit it for their own gain. But here's the thing. The ocean doesn't have a say in the matter. *You do.* And so does your father."

Phil picked up two paint cans. "But… it is *very* seductive. All of that attention and money. Pander to *that* audience, and you *will* lose yourself." He gave a jerk of his head. "C'mon. Let's go get some red."

Kyle and Phil climbed down and leaned into Phil's open trunk. Suddenly, the sound of sirens howled in the distance. Kyle exchanged a panicked look with his uncle.

"What'd I tell you about the future, Kyle?"

Phil pulled keys out of his pants pocket and tossed them to Kyle.

"Let's go! You drive."

"I can't drive! I don't have a license!"

Phil ignored him and jumped in the passenger side.

Kyle shook his head. What more could go wrong?

"Hurry up! Let's go!"

Kyle panicked and jumped in. He fumbled around for the ignition, distracted by blue lights flashing wildly in the rearview mirror. He finally got the powerful engine roaring, threw it into gear, and peeled out.

Kyle glanced at the approaching lights through the side view mirror, looked up and… "Holy crap!" A wide-eyed raccoon raised on its hind legs, almost as if it was waving at he and Uncle Phil.

Kyle cut the wheel to avoid hitting the nocturnal bandit and lost control.

The Ferrari flew over the curb and crashed into artfully sculpted hedges.

The police cruiser slammed to a stop. The officer walked tentatively to Phil's car, flashlight pointed at Kyle. Kyle stared straight ahead, strangling the steering wheel. He still wasn't wearing a shirt.

"License and registration."

Kyle looked at Phil. He was *so dead* when his dad found out about this. The officer leaned down, peeked in, and raised an eyebrow at Kyle's bare chest. Phil, meanwhile, relaxed, eyes closed. Kyle didn't know if he was meditating or what.

"Kid, how *high* are you?"

Phil's eyes popped open. He leaned over and looked up at the policeman.

"No officer. You've got it mixed up. It's… Hi kid! How are *you*?!"

Kyle watched the officer stiffen. He called for backup, and then proceeded to tell them both to get out of the car, leaving their hands where the officer could see them.

Peter drove through the night, trying not to speed, but feeling fury and terror at the same time—a sensation he did *not* appreciate. Red-eyed, grim, he glanced in his rearview mirror, and wiped a stray tear.

He grabbed his phone, scrolled down to "Sam" and hesitated. It was the middle of the night. He looked up at the road, paused, then pressed "Call."

"Peter?" Her voice registered worry. "Is everything okay?"

Peter tried to collect himself. He was afraid his voice might crack.

"Peter? Can you hear me?"

"I'm sorry, Sam." He swallowed. "I'm heading to the police station. Phil and Kyle are there. There was an accident. I didn't know who to call."

"Oh my, God! Are they OK?"

"Not hurt, but… they're in lockup. Downtown."

"I'll head right over!"

The line went dead. Peter drove on, arriving at the downtown station.

It was a busy night. Drunks and drug addicts, screaming men and women protesting their innocence or pleading for methadone. Peter found the desk sergeant, who told him where to wait. Peter sat hunched over, hands clasped, staring at the floor.

He lost track of time until he heard a familiar voice in the cacophony of misery that was a downtown L.A. police station on a weekend night. "Peter!"

He looked up and spied Sam rushing towards him. He slowly stood. Sam flew into his arms. Peter held her tight, grateful as relief flooded through him. His ex was in Monterey for the weekend, and he didn't want to freak her out until he had all the facts—not to mention they would have no doubt fought like they seemed to be so good at. Sam smelled of a citrus perfume, and she rubbed his back. Peter suddenly caught himself and returned to "boss" role.

He pulled away, put his hand on her back, and steered her to the exit so they could talk away from the insanity.

Once outside on the sidewalk, Peter lost it, "I can't believe he did this. And now he's dragging my *kid* into his shit?! I honestly thought that once he got established, on a new track, he'd be okay. But I guess a leopard doesn't change his spots."

"Peter, I understand you're upset—"

"You're goddamn right I'm upset!"

"Well then."

"Look, this could really fuck up Kyle's life. How many med schools are gonna welcome a kid with a record? Do you know what kind of a check I'm going to have to cut a big-time law firm to make this shit go away?"

"I understand, but be grateful that they're both okay. I mean—"

Peter laughed sarcastically. "Oh, yeah, I'm so *fucking* grateful! I've sacrificed everything for *both* of them, and *now* look what I'm dealing with—"

"Wow!" Sam's mouth literally dropped open.

"Wow, what?!"

"Really? Is *everything* about you? They could've been killed, and you're crying about *you*? Your sacrifices? You're the one who created this whole scene, and now you can't believe it's blowing up in your face!"

Sam audibly exhaled as if she was trying to control her temper. But then she raised her voice louder. "You know, you screwed up Phil's childhood, then doubled down and exploited his amnesia, and—"

"What did you just say to me?" Peter put his hands on his hips, stunned.

"You know, it would be comical if it weren't so damn sad. And now you're writing *Kyle's* story, oblivious to what *he* wants. It's all about you. How Peter looks. What's in it for Peter. It doesn't matter to you in the *least* what anyone else wants. And you wonder why everyone leaves."

"You just don't get it, do you?" Peter poked his index finger at her. "I've failed with Phil. I just need to accept that *Phil* is who he is. A self-destructive fuckup, who will never amount to anything. I've given him an opportunity of a lifetime, made him successful—"

Sam laughed, throwing her hands up to muffle it, but kept laughing bitterly.

"You wanna let me in on the joke?"

She composed herself. "It just *hit* me. You don't know. You're honestly stumped as to why Phil is 'self-destructive,' as you put it. Sure, it appears to the world like he has a perfect life. But it's not what HE wants. His new life is *your* perception of perfect."

"What are you *talking about*?"

"I can't believe I didn't see this before. You think a person isn't complete unless they've 'made it.' You even used the word 'amount.' Phil won't 'amount' to anything. I mean, look at *your* life. All of the trappings of wealth and celebrity, and you know what the irony is? You've created a façade... of a perfect and happy life, and you're one of the unhappiest people I know. People only see you on stage. They have no idea how empty you are behind the curtain. And that's the sad reality of who *you've* become. You aren't the same man I believed in when I went to work for you."

Peter's emotions careened from stunned, to hurt, to pissed off. He looked directly at Sam, who looked away.

"Those were shitty things to say. I'm glad I know how you *really* feel."

She returned her gaze to his face. Her eyes flashed fury. "Please spare me the woe-is-me act.

You just can't stand to hear the truth because it shatters your illusion that you're perfect. Well, you're not. No one is. And you know something else? I've had enough of you and your shit! I'm done!"

Peter could not believe this was happening—on one of the worst nights of his life. "Are you kidding me?"

Sam looked at him, an expression of pity and disgust on her face, then turned and walked away.

"Sam! Hold on a minute," he called out after her.

Sam stopped and turned around.

"I… I need you." He couldn't believe he was admitting it.

Sam walked slowly towards Peter, stopped and looked expectantly up at his eyes, her eyes darting one to the other, trying to read his emotions.

Peter pleaded. "You're the only one who can manage Dan."

Sam stared at him incredulously. Shaking her head sadly, fury still in her eyes, she turned, walked away, jumped in her Jeep, and screeched her tires as she left the police parking lot in a rush.

Peter returned to the police station. He was able to get Kyle released, but told the officers that his brother could stay there and rot.

Kyle eventually was handed over to Peter.

"Where the fuck is your shirt?"

"Keats needed it. For a painting," Kyle whispered, head hanging low.

"You know what? I don't ever want to hear the name Keats again. And for that matter, *you* are not to speak the entire ride home. I don't want to hear your bullshit story of how this happened. So I'm going to do all the talking the whole ride—and you will shut up."

With that, he grabbed Kyle by the arm and pulled him out of the noisy station.

On Monday, Peter stood, exhausted, at his treadmill desk. He rifled through his mail and stopped at an envelope hand-addressed to "Peter."

He removed Sam's letter of resignation, glanced at it, sighed, then lifted up and read a handwritten note:

*Dear Peter, Phil turned me on to the poet Rumi. I think you'll appreciate this. And good luck Peter. I really mean it.*

*Very little grows on jagged rock.*
*Be ground. Be crumbled.*

*So wildflowers will come up*
*Where you are.*
*You have been stony for too many years.*
*Try something different. Surrender.*

Peter stared at the poem then glanced at Sam's empty desk, feeling an unfamiliar pain in his chest.

At home in his bedroom Friday night, Peter leaned over his drafting table, and scanned his father's unfinished children's book. He picked up some colored pencils nearby and started sketching.

He turned the sheet. *What's this?!* Someone had written a surprising, poetic passage on one of the illustrations.

*Hmm… that handwriting looks familiar.*

Peter glanced out the window. Phil rolled up very slowly in his Ferrari, stopped and parked across the street.

From downstairs, Kyle shouted, "I'm heading to Jonesy's to study."

Peter felt like a bull, and his brother's Ferrari was the red cape. He'd put a stop to this crap.

"Oh, yeah? Okay, check in with me later."

"Will do, Dad," came the response.

There was more than one way to skin a cat—and catch someone in a lie. Peter peeked out the window and watched Kyle's escape with Phil. *Why was Kyle so damn fascinated by his flakey brother?*

Peter raced downstairs, opting for the grey Mercedes—the Tesla was a dead giveaway, and he never drove the Mercedes. He pulled onto the street a safe distance from them and followed his brother's car with his damn kid in the passenger seat.

Eventually, they pulled in front of a nightclub. *He's underage!*

The sign illuminated the block:

## APPEARING TONIGHT
## MOON

Peter walked in the front door and scanned the dark, crowded club. He could not believe his kid was here when he was grounded from just about anything but studying for eternity.

A band was setting up, moving instruments, and doing a sound-check.

Peter finally spotted the back of Phil's white, spiked head seated at a small table facing the stage.

He walked over, casually pulled up a chair, and sat facing Phil. They stared at each other.

Behind Peter, Moon's band was getting warmed up. A slow click, click, click of the drumsticks, followed by a slow, deep bass guitar. And then... loud, screeching guitar feedback, followed by silence.

Peter spun around and was shocked to see Kyle on stage, staring down at his guitar, his face completely crestfallen. His son looked at his hands, finger-picked a few notes, off-key again, then froze.

Defeated, head hanging.

Moon motioned the band to stop playing. *The poor kid*.

Peter turned to Phil, eyes full of rage and anguish.

"You fucking asshole!"

"What, *Dad*?"

"Can't you see my kid isn't *ready* for this? That your encouraging him in some fucking pipe dream, the way you've lived your whole Keats-ian dream-life?"

Peter wanted to jump across the table and strangle Phil. He held in his anger and stood. "Fuck you, *Bro*."

He walked towards the exit.

He paused and glanced back at the stage. Moon took off his signature hat and placed it on Kyle's head.

"Let it go, baby. Let it play *you*. Remember… you think, you stink."

Kyle nodded. Moon removed Kyle's glasses and placed his dark sunglasses on Kyle. He nodded at the band to start it up again.

Peter fumed more. Without his glasses, Kyle was blind as a bat. Ridiculous. This was all a cruel joke.

He turned and pushed his way past stunned, wide-eyed people, frozen in place. *What's wrong with these idiots?* He was almost intentionally not listening to what was happening on stage. It was too damn humiliating! He tried to move through the crowd, and then he *felt* it before he heard it. A riff. A mind-blowing virtuoso guitar solo, someone's fingers literally on fire moving up and down the strings.

Peter felt every hair on the nape of his neck rise. Perfect tone. Howling string bends. Something emotionally deep was happening. It had to be someone in Moon's band. *Oh… my… God! Is that Stevie Ray Vaughn reincarnated?!* A rockin', powerhouse blues guitar solo exploded through the club. Chills climbed up and down Peter's spine, and he finally forced himself to whirl around.

He turned his head slowly to the stage. The audience was standing, going wild! Moon smiled at the crowd, throwing up both arms as proof. *It ain't me playin'.*

Peter, drop-jawed, watched Kyle—his *son*—throw down chorus after chorus of haunting, penetrating licks to the end. Then he turned and left, blocking out the raucous round of applause.

Peter walked to his car. Behind him, he heard running footfall. Peter glanced over his shoulder. Phil had run out after him.

Peter whirled around, ready to scream at his brother, and was shocked to find that *Phil* looked furious at *him.*

"What the *hell* was that!? Your kid lays it all out there, and you walk *out*?! Are you fucking kidding me?!"

"You better back the fuck up. I *specifically* told you to leave him alone."

"Oh, right, I keep forgetting. YOU decide what everyone does. YOU'RE the one who writes everyone's story, like they're a fucking toaster oven.

I'm sorry for thinking he may want to do what HE wants to do."

"Don't push me. I mean it Phil."

"You know what's bothering you?"

"That YOU got my kid arrested?"

"No. You hate that the kid surprised you—you *hate* surprises. He didn't follow your fucking script!" Phil suddenly laughed and raised his eyebrows. "Your appliances can't surprise you, but people sure can, can't they?"

Peter kept his face stony.

"Okay then—" Phil got right in Peter's face. "How 'bout *this* for a surprise?!"

Phil stuck his index finger in his ear and aggressively wiggled it. Peter watched, confused.

*Wait. No. No. This can't be.* Peter's body shivered, as if a gust of a winter storm passed over him.

Paralyzed by the truth, he stammered and then took a step backwards.

"Are... *you* telling me you've had your memory this whole time?!"

Phil tilted his head to the right. "Pretty impressive performance, huh Pete?"

"You've been fucking playing me?!"

"*I've* been playing YOU?! Oh, that's a classic Peter Anderson if ever I heard one. We should maybe engrave that on a plaque or something."

Kyle walked out. Peter didn't even look at him.

"Get in the car."

"But Dad—"

Peter turned and stared him down. "NOW!"

*Abraham Maslow spoke of "peak experiences." You've asked me to write about what life events, people, etc. "inform" my music. Peak experiences are basically a simplified way of saying that you have had a moment—a peak experience—when every single star aligns in the sky, when you transcend the moment and become timeless yourself. My mother said the moment I came into the world, when I cried in the delivery room, that was her "mountaintop" experience that nothing else could compare to.*

*But on stage... that was my moment. Not the whole bad riff. After that. When I stopped thinking. In that moment on the stage I became my music. I left my thinking self far behind and became something, someone, else.*

*That was the best moment of my life.*

*The worst? Watching my dad and Uncle Phil become more estranged.*

*Oh, and I am sure you are pretty shocked, right? Yup. Keats deserved an Oscar.*

# Surrender

mnesiac or not, Keats was teaching me things. Well, he was also getting me into trouble. As things were shaping up, I would probably be grounded until I was retirement age.

But he was teaching me to figure out my own voice, who I was, what I wanted. And after playing that club, I knew my destiny, my joy, my passion with every single fiber in my being. And that I would have to defend it and protect it and... love it... to make sure I never lost sight of it, the way my dad was lost.

He also taught me that your "gift" is the spirit you bring to everyone you meet and everything you do. Before that night on stage, I definitely worked hard to learn to move my fingers so fast, to hear the circle of fifths and minor and major harmonies. But that moment was about *something a lot more powerful than being able to play the notes.*

*I left a part of me on that stage.*
*I gave it everything I had.*
*I bled for my art.*

The next afternoon Phil sat at the bar. Empty shot glasses lined up in front of him. He raised a glass to Moon, yelling out, "Hey Moon! You think, you stink!"

Moon peered at him, clearly thinking, *Crazy fool.*

Phil kept pounding expensive tequila shots. And fuming. *How could Peter still not get it?*

Fuck it. Time to raise the ante.

Peter looked at his watch. He was downstairs dressed in his favorite Tom Ford tux.

He called out, "Kyle, come down here please."

Kyle walked very slowly down the stairs, as if facing an executioner. He stood and glared at Peter, clearly pissed.

273

"I thought you'd like to know. Your hero? Uncle... Keats? Apparently, he's had his memory all along. That should make you pretty proud—"

"I already knew that."

Peter sputtered, "What?! How long have you known?"

"Pretty much from the beginning."

"Oh my God... you were his accomplice in this charade?"

"Seriously, Dad? If anyone should be disappointed in someone, it should be me and uncle Phil... in *you*."

"What?! Do you have any idea what kind of problems he's created for me? For you?! I've sacrificed everything for you... for both of you, and this is the thanks I get?"

"You know, Dad, for someone as smart as you..." He shook his head. "Uncle Phil never wanted what *you* wanted. But that didn't really matter to you, did it?!"

Peter couldn't believe his ears! This *kid*, who was grounded, was acting like the wronged party. He was sticking up for *Keats*!

"And I never wanted to go to med school! OK!"

Peter stared at him blankly. He was so tired of fighting this. He just wanted his old life when it all went according to plan. He sighed. "I get it."

Then he turned and left, defeated.

❧

Peter stood and walked to the podium in the hotel's grand ballroom. The black-tie fundraiser celebrated a non-profit anniversary—art programs in inner-city schools.

Round, white linen covered tables filled the room. Champagne was being served in elegant flutes all around. A ten-tiered cake was displayed up front, near a podium. A poster on an easel read:

## ENLIGHTEN UP FOR CREATIVITY WITH PETER ANDERSON

At Peter's front VIP table, Dan sat with Peter, Ramona, and other muckety-mucks. Peter's heart dipped. Sam should have been there.

Lights dimmed, the room quieted. Peter adjusted his jacket, and stepped to the podium to applause.

Peter nodded. "Thank you. And thank you, everyone, for being here, and for being involved with such a worthy cause. And thank you Dan for inviting me to speak."

Dan shot Peter a look that said, *I've got you by the balls. Time for you to dance.*

Peter stared out on the wider audience. "Matisse wrote, 'Creativity takes courage.' I certainly know *that* to be true. I've been working with a dedicated team for more than three years to create something amazing… something we can all be proud of. And even as I speak to you today, our very survival is in question. But… we *embrace* this chaos. We *relish* the unknown. Because we've built a supportive community. A fearless space of collaborative creativity—"

Suddenly, from the back of the room, a mocking voice called out, "Bullshit!" like a sneeze. Peter squinted through the bright lights. He could not make out his detractor. Maybe it was a sneeze. Maybe he was imagining things after this shit storm of a week.

"By letting go of hierarchical, command-and-control management and placing *trust* in my people, I've learned that—"

"Fuckin' hypocrite!"

Patrons turned, looking toward the back with disgust. Peter shuffled his notes to finish and get off the stage. He did not need a heckler and hoped security would escort the jerk out.

"Picasso said, 'Art is the lie that enables us to realize the truth'—"

The heckler shouted, "Then you should change your *name* to Art... asshole, 'cause you're a big lie. How come you can't see it?"

*Who is that?!*

Phil stepped into the light, gestured to the crowd, and stumbled toward the podium. "And ya know what? Neither can any of these other fine... sheeple."

Peter finally saw him in the midst of the crowd, coming closer. He stared at Phil like a soldier eyeing the enemy. Phil weaved a few more steps, bumped into a VIP table, spilling drinks all around. The patrons recoiled, shocked.

Peter stepped around from the podium, realizing once again he would have to clean up his brother's mess and get him the hell out of there. But as he walked towards his brother, he slipped on the spill Phil created and fell into the immense cake.

Phil broke out in laughter.

Peter jumped up, covered in frosting. Despite the shock of a heckler at an elegant nonprofit fundraiser, Peter could hear the audience snickering.

That was it!

Peter lunged furiously and grabbed Phil by the lapels of his jacket, and tried to drag him out a side door, whispering fury under this breath, "You are dead!"

The showy crowd was horrified. Frenzied photographers flashed shots. Phil grabbed Peter and whipped him back onto the toppled cake.

Peter could barely see or breathe, he was so enraged. He rose to his feet, turned, and tackled Phil. Phil turned Peter over, kneeling on top of him.

Dan ran over and grabbed Phil by the shoulders, shouting the words: "You fuckin' moron! This is *Big Dan's* fundraiser!"

Dan turned and hauled back to sucker punch Phil. Suddenly, Peter jumped up, catching Dan's arm. Peter turned to Phil—his *brother*—then spun and drilled Dan in the mouth, knocking him to the floor. He connected so hard, his knuckles hurt.

Peter looked down at Dan. Dan, stunned, wiped blood from his lip, then looked up at Peter, rage in his eyes.

Peter gave Dan a pensive stare.

Phil leaned in, looking down at Dan. "So Big Dan? Has anyone mentioned that the negative space between your ears codifies the exploration of your utter stupidity?"

Peter, covered in cake and gasping for air, grabbed Phil by the jacket and dragged him out the side door.

Out in a back parking lot, Peter and Phil stood side by side, hunched over and out of breath. Suddenly, Peter started to laugh. It slowly turned maniacal.

Phil stared at him.

Peter finally caught his breath. "That's the first time I've laughed, *really* laughed, in a long time."

"No shit. What the hell's so funny?"

"God, did you make an ass out of me. I mean, the whole time it *felt* like you were... *screwing* with me. But I kept thinking, why would he do that to me? It just didn't make sense. And it makes even less sense now."

He looked right at Phil's cake-covered face. "Why would you cause me so much grief? I've done *nothing* but try to help you our entire lives."

"Really?" Phil asked. "First off, YOU made the ass of yourself. Okay? And you still really don't get it, do you?"

Phil. Sam. Kyle. They all kept asking the same question of him. "Get what, damn it?"

"You've done nothing BUT try to 'help me' my whole life. I wasn't your little brother. I was your management project. And I was never what you wanted me to be."

Peter squinted.

"You honestly don't understand what I was doing, do you? For the first time in MY life, I felt like I was in control. I felt like I had a voice. And I wanted you to feel how emasculated and powerless I've felt since mom and dad died! YOU picked my major. YOU picked the college I went to. YOU decided how and where we would celebrate every holiday."

"You hate me that much, Phil? Don't you understand that all the things I've done for you, I did because I wanted the best for you?"

"It doesn't matter if I understood it. What matters is that I didn't feel like you—" Phil turned away and swallowed hard. "—like you loved me."

Peter was stunned. He could not remember Phil being emotional like this since they were children.

"You never talked about them... ever." Phil's voice quavered. "Do you know for years, I thought that you didn't even care? We never once went back to the loft. We never even visited their graves."

Tears hung from Phil's eyes, threatening to spill.

Peter said softly, earnestly, "Phil, I didn't know *what* to do. I... I just wanted to protect you. I thought that it would be more painful if we talked about them. I didn't know."

Peter looked down at the ground.

Phil's voice was hoarse. "All I *wanted*... was my big brother to tell me it was going to be okay. And you never did." The tears spilled and the sobs wrenched his voice. "Do you know that after the funeral you never—" Phil gulped at air, as if a dam of unshed tears had burst. "—you never even *touched* me again?"

Peter looked up, eyes wide, tears welling up. He grabbed Phil and forcefully pulled him in. Phil's eyes registered shock. Then he threw his arms around Peter. They held each other, cake-covered, crying, in the hotel parking lot.

"I'm so sorry. I really am... I love you, Phil."

Phil's eyes warmed. He closed them as tears continued to flood out.

"I love you too."

After a long embrace, Peter's shoulders sagged. "I'm so tired, Phil."

He clapped his brother on the back. "I've been a *perfect* fool." Peter released his hug, but still held Phil by the shoulders, looking into Phil's eyes and smiling.

Phil reached out, wiped frosting from Peter's face. Then raised his hand to his mouth, ate the frosting, raised his eyebrows and smiled.

Phil said, "Nobody's perfect, bro. Not even you."

Ramona, frantic, burst out of the building. She stepped into the evening air, finding Peter with an arm around Phil. Peter wiped his tears, smiled, gestured to Ramona and pulled her in with his free hand. All three embraced.

Peter whispered, "Thank you for everything… mamá."

Ramona released a guttural sob and patted his arm.

Finally, Peter said, "I'm okay now." He looked into Phil's eyes. "*We're* OK."

Phil and Peter each kissed Ramona on the cheek and walked arm in arm towards the parking lot.

"Here I was thinking I was going to change *your* story… give you a second chance. And you're the one who changed *mine*."

"*You* changed it, bro. I just added a few plot twists. 'Cause ya' know… nothing really *means* anything until you've experienced it." He grinned. "And speaking of experiences… I got you something *really special* for *your* birthday. I'd like to give it to you a little early."

Peter looked down at his tux. "I'm a mess."

The two of them climbed into Phil's car. Phil reached into the back. "Here. Use this rag to get that icing off of you."

Peter nodded and tried not to wonder where his brother was taking him. Twenty minutes later they pulled up to a storefront. Above the space, a sign read: "Dionysus Dance."

"You know I don't dance. What's this?"

"It's exactly what you need. Come on."

The two brothers walked into the dance studio. Quiet and empty, Peter could see that the studio was just getting off the ground—boxes and confusion were in the office. Phil and Peter stood together on the glistening dance floor.

Behind him he heard a voice. *Her* voice. "Hello? Can I help you?" Phil rubbed Peter's back.

"Happy Birthday, bro. I'll catch up with you later."

Phil walked out of the studio, then Peter finally felt his courage gather. He turned around. Sam walked out.

He stood, arms folded across his chest, wearing his cake-encrusted tux, some stray icing here and there on his face and in his hair.

Sam, in an incredibly sexy bodysuit, with a sarong, her hair loose, barefoot, walked closer to him, looking him up and down and taking in his Tux, then stared tenderly into his eyes."

Peter dropped his arms, looked deeply into Sam's eyes, and whispered, "I surrender."

Sam lunged forward and threw her arms around him. They kissed passionately. Peter thought it was the kind of kiss you would remember on your deathbed.

Sam pulled back and licked her lips. "Butter cream?"

They laughed and then embraced. Peter stared intensely into her eyes.

Suddenly, Peter's phone buzzed in his pants pocket against Sam. She looked down, then back up into his eyes. She offered him a sexy, flirtatious smile, then winked. "Go ahead... take it."

Peter pulled out his phone. It was a text from Phil.

I AM REALLY PROUD OF YOU. <3

Tears welled up in Peter's eyes. He texted back:

NO, I AM PROUD OF YOU! <3 <3 <3

On Monday, Peter sat at the head of the conference room table, head down sketching a big white cat, oblivious to the gloom and doom in the room.

Peter's advisory board, serious business-types, were huddled next to Dan. Zack was at the far end of the table, as usual enjoying his bagel.

Grave and stern, the business types took turns dressing Peter down for the fundraiser disaster, the movie schedule slippage, and the company's financial performance.

All except Zack, who was at the other end of the table, leaning back, smiling, and scarfing down another bagel.

Suddenly, Peter stopped drawing, opened his briefcase, placed the drawing and other documents inside, closed it, and stood.

He spoke calmly—and was shocked that he actually *felt* calm. "Thank you all for everything. I wish you the very best."

With that, Peter walked out, leaving Dan and the suits sputtering fury, and Zack grinning from ear to ear.

An hour later, Ramona walked in and sat across from Peter. Peter placed his photo of Kyle into a cardboard box.

"Ramona, Phil and I need one more favor from you."

Peter picked up a check from his desk and handed it to her.

Ramona looked at it. Stunned by the amount.

"Yeah, I know. Zack just walked in here and wrote the damn thing. His exact words were, 'Nothing ventured, nothing will happen.'"

Peter shook his head, grinned. "Who would have guessed?"

Ramona smiled.

"He also bought out Dan, just gave him what he wanted, so we don't have to deal with *him* anymore."

"So are you staying then? Why are you packing?"

"No, I'm not stayin'. Phil and I have invested everything we have left in the company and, with Zack, we've made *you* the new CEO. We want *you* to finish the film. Find its heart and make it great. And if your contribution is even a fraction of what you've done for us, it will be an *estupendo* success."

Ramona stood, teary-eyed. She pulled Peter into a warm hug.

"Thank you, *mi hijo*."

Peter just smiled, and, whistling, took his box of belongings and walked out of the company he had built.

On Saturday afternoon, Phil and Peter relaxed at a table, drinking coffees. Kyle, wearing Phil's old Neil Young T-shirt, played guitar on stage. Jonesy banged on drums, and a cute African-American girl played bass. Kyle looked at her and smiled—a lot.

Peter leaned over and asked Phil, "Who's the girl? She's incredible."

"That's Moon's granddaughter, Jade. I guess they're right about talent running in the family. Huh, bro."

Phil smiled. The blues song ended. Peter yelled to the stage. "You guys know any Neil Young?" He pointed to his brother. "Huge fan here."

Kyle looked at Peter and Phil and smiled. Peter smiled back and winked. He was amazed at Kyle's transformation. Not only did his son have more confidence, but their relationship had utterly changed—it was easy now, with genuine openness. And damn but Kyle glowed. He was so happy, sometimes Peter wondered if the kid's feet even touched the ground.

They stayed for the rest of the set, then Phil and Peter stood up and walked out, messing with each other as best friends. Peter rubbed Phil's head. Phil punched him in the arm.

"When are you going to drop the Billy Idol look, there Keats?"

"When are you going to drop the 'stick up your ass' look, Coleridge?"

"You have to admit. I'm working on it."

From the café, they drove to the cemetery. Phil and Peter stood side by side, looking down at their parents' graves.

Peter handed Phil a bouquet of flowers. Phil unscrewed the lid to his Superman thermos, placed the flowers inside and gently set it down against the headstone.

The day had finally arrived. Samantha rushed around her condo lighting candles, putting the finishing touches on the event.

The invite had read:

*JOIN US FOR A BOOK SIGNING*
*with Phil Anderson (writer) and*
*Peter Anderson (illustrator)*

Black and white balloons filled the room. A few dozen chairs set up facing a fireplace. The caterers laid out appetizers on her dining room table.

Shortly, guests arrived and soon were milling around, drinking wine. Sam and Kyle handed out copies of Peter and Phil's (and their father's) children's book.

Zack stood at the table of food, wearing a Hawaiian shirt and stuffing his face. A woman turned to Zack.

"So how do you know the authors?"

Zack kept chewing. "Oh, I knew Pete in another life."

Sam, overhearing them, just smiled. She had known him in another life too. And now in this new life. It was a miracle.

The condo was full, and Sam grabbed Kyle away from his new girlfriend, Jade.

The two of them approached the brothers, who were sitting side-by-side on a sofa. "Time to do the reading and signing."

Phil placed his hand on Peter's knee and pushed himself to his feet. He looked at Sam and Kyle, then past them, wide-eyed, to a flash of blackness on Sam's balcony. Its sleek body, like ebony, settling on the deck railing, head tilted to the side.

"Umm… Pete?"

Peter sat cuddling and stroking Vincent, Sam's big, white cat and the inspiration for their children's book. He looked up at Phil.

"Yeah. What's up, bro?"

Phil watched as the crow spread its wings and flew away, its iridescent feathers catching the sunlight. He rolled his eyes, drew a deep breath and turned towards the crowd gathered in the living room.

"Never mind. It's... nothin'."

Peter reached out, snagged Phil's arm and gave it a squeeze. He nodded his head as he looked down at his brother's hand. Then he looked directly into Phil's eyes.

"I know bro. They're... beautiful!"

Phil smiled widely and nodded, knowingly. Then he stepped towards the fireplace at the front of the room.

Peter stood, turned to Kyle, handed him the cat and smiled. He wrapped his arms around Kyle's shoulders and kissed him. Then he turned and faced the crowd.

Without Vincent in his arms, cat hair covered Peter's clothes, and the white lettering on his black T-shirt was visible.

## I AM KEATS

A huge smile washed over Peter's face.

The reading went well. Sam beamed, Zack milled around the food and drinks, and Kyle and Jade were nowhere to be found.

Afterwards, Peter glanced at Phil. They were surrounded by autograph-seekers. Phil looked uncomfortable. He glanced at Peter, raised his eyebrows, put his finger in his ear and wiggled it.

Peter, eyes wet, smiled broadly, nodding. Phil returned the smile and nodded.

The two brothers no longer needed words.

Their connection was on another level.

One that was inside of them all along.

*So we've arrived at the end of our story.*

*I have to apologize for not letting on that I knew Uncle Phil really didn't have amnesia. If I had told you that, well, you wouldn't have taken this journey with me.*

*I know this is a crazy story. I told you—Tolstoy understood that all unhappy families are unhappy in their own unique way. And I can promise you, my family's story is about as crazy and unique as they come.*

*But here's what I learned. And how it informs my music.*

*First, life and stories are very close, but like guitar strings they never actually touch. We don't write our stories. Life does. So it doesn't matter what we tell ourselves. What matters is how we live. As John Keats himself said, "There is nothing stable in the world; uproar's your only music." And if we're in tune with ourselves, we're in tune with the world.*

*So we've got to trust that "still, small voice" that speaks truth. We need to speak our gifts aloud. We need to go with the flow of the Universe and steer our own ship. And we need to not let other people's stories steer us into the rocks, like the call of the Sirens.*

*And that applies to music. Let yourself be the music. If you think—it stinks.*

*If you need a real example, think about when Bob Dylan went electric. Levon Helm, of "The Band" (brilliant in his own right) once said he had never heard of Dylan. But Dylan had heard of The Band. Try to imagine that! Bob asked them if they wanted to play The Hollywood Bowl with him. And what a wild, unscripted ride that was. It was what they called in the sixties a "happening." And it almost didn't happen. Sometimes, you just have to jump on the train and let the wind blow through your hair, living like a tramp. Living a life built on moments of serendipity.*

*Second, I really, really want to go to your school to study music. But if you don't choose me, I will be disappointed but ultimately OK with it because while I know I can learn a great deal at your conservatory, I also know that I don't need anyone to tell me I am a musician—and a damn good one. The applause is awesome. But I play for me. (And the fact that Jade digs it doesn't hurt.)*

*Third, I learned all about the importance of balance. Yin and yang. Passion and planning. Keats and Coleridge. And I discovered that to live a rich, full and meaningful life, to be truly alive, I need to let Keats drive me and use Coleridge as my pit crew, to keep me well-maintained and help me stay alive.*

*Finally, I realize that I need to grab the moments. The peak experiences. Those precious times when the Universe aligns and you find yourself living in the sacred air above the humdrum, the ordinary. But here is the other secret— you can access those moments all the time. And that's when music is made. Real music. Mozart and Beethoven, to Moon to Muddy Waters to… Ella and Lady Day.*

*Uncle Phil had been trying to tell me that my whole life. When he taught me to fly on my bike, he was showing me to not force it, to just let the wind lift you, and then soar. My fingers soar on the strings now. As if they have a life of their own.*

*Oh. One last thing.*

*Remember how I said I was an only child? Well, Sam and my dad are expecting—a girl. Uncle Phil tells Dad he's going to teach her how to ride a bike, and Sam says she is going to teach her to dance.*

*But me? My little sister is going to know she can do anything she wants. She can do anything, be anything, go anywhere. She will learn that life is uncertain. But love is never uncertain.*

*And I have a feeling the day I meet her will be a peak experience.*

## AUTHORS' NOTE
### On Keats and Coleridge

We didn't purposely set out to use two 19th century English Romantic poets as metaphors for the novel's central characters and their distinctly different predispositions toward life. Who in their right minds would, right? But we weren't *in* our right minds when we created *I am Keats*; we were possessed by something much larger than ourselves. Like just about everything else in the story, it mysteriously happened all on its own.

In the very beginning of the writing process, which began as a screenplay, the brothers began to "speak" to us, with resolve, like blades of grass trying to push through our analytical asphalt. And as we allowed them to slowly come to life, we started to notice a curious parallel to a duality of mind. Phil was embodying the *feeling* mind—spontaneity, uncertainty, and experience. And Peter was the quintessential *thinking* mind—order, control, and progress.

During that time, we stumbled upon the passionate poetry and life of John Keats and, shortly thereafter, Samuel Taylor Coleridge. Keats was attracted to the real and tangible; the sensuous sights and sounds of nature, as well as the joys and suffering of mankind. Coleridge was driven more by thoughts and reflections, philosophical musing and intellectual abstraction; the representative and instructive nature of the world.

That serendipitous encounter with two dead poets felt so strangely "right" to us that Keats and Coleridge became Phil and Peter. But they also turned into a powerful ontological metaphor; a model of the mind. And as we ventured deeper into the writing process, that model eventually took over *our* minds, informing our work and our lives. It's one strange story, and you can read more about it and the various philosophies that emerged at www.iamkeats.com/keats-and-coleridge, and in the companion book *I am Keats: Escape Your Mind and Free Your Self.*

In addition to the Keats/Coleridge metaphor, other weird, unintended elements wrote themselves into the story. We only became aware of many of them after the fact, details like the symbolism of the crow, and the meaning of the characters names. We discovered Peter means "stone" and Phil means "lover"—a *phil*osopher is a lover of wisdom. And

Samantha means "listener" and Ramona means "protecting hands."

There's also the yin yang connection, the interdependent relationship of opposing but complementary forces that give rise to each other through their interaction. In this dynamic tension of forces, Phil personifies yin and Peter represents yang. And there's Peter leaving his studio, Apollo, and ending up at Sam's dance studio, Dionysus, which is a reference to Nietzsche's philosophical dichotomy drawn from Greek mythology. The Apollonian culture and archetype values order and harmony, and favors reason and rational thinking over feeling and intuition. By contrast, the Dionysian essence is a celebration of our chaotic nature, and the ecstasy and unique contribution to the world found in creativity and self-transformation.

We're sure there are other hidden meanings in the story, and we'd love to hear from you if you discover more. In the meantime, we want to thank you very much for reading our story. And thank you for taking the time to join the conversation online, post reviews, and to share on Facebook and Twitter and the rest. Really… thank you for everything. It means the world to us.

# DISCUSSION QUESTIONS

1.  The narrator, Kyle, talks about how "the blues" will bring every single person to their knees at one point in life. He says only each person's determination to rise up will decide whether they overcome or not. How is this a metaphor for obstacles in life? And is there a way to avoid obstacles and pain, or are they inevitable and perhaps even necessary?

2.  Peter is referred to as the poet "Coleridge" by his brother, and as "the man with the plan"? What do you think the authors are conveying about life's "best-laid plans"?

3.  Phil, the free-spirited brother, embraces the persona of Keats. What do you think attracts him to the poet Keats?

4.  The authors introduce the radical idea that our stories define us and confine us—often to our detriment. Do you agree with this? And what stories have you told yourself that now,

perhaps, you feel differently about?

5. What memories, do you feel, hold you prisoner? What would it mean for your life if you could magically "forget" them? Would you want to?

6. What do you think the authors are trying to convey about risk? "Keats" encourages Sam and Kyle to both embrace big risks. Is this practical? Why or why not?

7. What do you think the authors are trying to say about potential "failure"? How do you measure success or failure? Has the book changed your perception of success?

8. After the death of their parents, Peter thought that avoiding thinking about or discussing the tragedy was somehow the best way to face the loss. How can this view of difficult times be dangerous? When people don't share sorrow, can it drive them apart?

9.  Phil talks about the danger of conforming to what your audience expects. How does this intersect with the world of business, in terms of expectations? What does this say about creativity and innovation?

10. Phil tells Kyle to never forget, "You are *not* what you think others think of you." But Peter seems to believe the opposite when he tells Sam, "We end up becoming an accumulation of everyone else's ideas of who they think we are, of who we should be." Who do you think is right?

11. The book seems to be saying to follow your passion without concern for outcome. What passions could you see yourself exploring after reading the book?

12. "If you think, you stink," says Moon. Is this true? Why or why not?

13. Have you ever felt you were living the life someone else planned for you, as Kyle felt with his father pushing him to go on a

medical school track? What would change if you were to reject others' influence on your decisions?

14. In their note at the end of the book, the authors disclose that most of the story of *I am Keats* mysteriously wrote itself through them. What do you think: transcendent inspiration or creative intuition? And have you ever had a similar experience, with something greater than yourself?

## ABOUT THE AUTHORS

Tom Asacker is often described as a creative force, albeit a wayward one. He is an artist, writer, inventor, and philosopher. He writes, teaches, and speaks about radically new practices and ideas for success in times of uncertainty and change.

Shannon McCarthy-Minuti is a writer, designer, serial entrepreneur and professional chef. She loves dark humor and is the comedic voice of *I am Keats*.

*For more information, please visit their website at:*

*www.iamkeats.com*

CPSIA information can be obtained
at www.ICGtesting.com
Printed in the USA
LVOW13s1511210118
563427LV00027B/1539/P

9 781546 431305